WOMEN HAVE HEARTS

In the light from the candles and the moonlight outside, Kelda saw an expression in Lord Orsett's eyes that made her heart start beating furiously and she could not look away.

"I want your heart," he began. "I want it more than I have ever wanted anything . . ."

Because of the pain in his voice, Kelda was no longer afraid. "You . . . you want . . . me?" she asked.

"I have loved you from the moment I saw you, but I told myself it was an illusion . . ." Lord Orsett said positively. "Tell me what I want to hear. Say it, darling!"

"I love . . . you!" she whispered. But the words were lost as Lord Orsett's lips came down on hers, holding her captive. Now there was only him, and he filled the world and the sky.

Bantam Books by Barbara Cartland
Ask your bookseller for the books you have missed

6 THE BORED BRIDE-
  GROOM
20 THE FLAME IS LOVE
46 THE INCREDIBLE
  HONEYMOON
69 THE DRAGON AND THE
  PEARL
73 THE NAKED BATTLE
76 THE CASTLE MADE
  FOR LOVE
78 THE SAINT AND THE
  SINNER
79 A FUGITIVE FROM
  LOVE
80 THE TWISTS AND TURNS
  OF LOVE
81 THE PROBLEMS OF
  LOVE
82 LOVE LEAVES AT
  MIDNIGHT
83 MAGIC OR MIRAGE

92 THE RACE FOR LOVE
98 THE DRUMS OF LOVE
99 ALONE IN PARIS
100 THE PRINCE AND THE
  PEKINGESE
101 THE SERPENT OF
  SATAN
102 THE TREASURE IS LOVE
103 LIGHT OF THE MOON
104 THE PRISONER OF LOVE
105 FLOWERS FOR THE GOD
  OF LOVE
106 A VOICE IN THE DARK
108 LOVE CLIMBS IN
109 A NIGHTINGALE SANG
110 TERROR IN THE SUN
111 WHO CAN DENY LOVE?
112 LOVE HAS HIS WAY
113 THE EXPLOSION OF LOVE
114 ONLY LOVE
115 WOMEN HAVE HEARTS

Barbara Cartland's Library of Love series

RAMAZAN THE RAJAH
THE MONEY MOON
THE ROCKS OF VALPRE

Books of Love and Revelation
THE TREASURE OF HO

Other Books by Barbara Cartland

I SEEK THE MIRACULOUS

Women Have Hearts

Barbara Cartland

BANTAM BOOKS
TORONTO · NEW YORK · LONDON

WOMEN HAVE HEARTS
A Bantam Book | January 1980

ISBN 0–553–13446–9

Published simultaneously in the United States and Canada

Bantam Books are published by Bantam Books, Inc. Its trade-mark, consisting of the words "Bantam Books" and the por-trayal of a bantam, is Registered in U.S. Patent and Trademark Office and in other countries. Marca Registrada. Bantam Books, Inc., 666 Fifth Avenue, New York, New York 10019.

PRINTED IN THE UNITED STATES OF AMERICA

DESIGNED BY MIERRE

Author's Note

Dakar, which rapidly became the centre of colonial society in the twentieth century, required a lot of construction and public works to make the living conditions suitable for Europeans. From 125 European merchants and company employees in 1900, the white population of Dakar rose to 2,500 in 1910.

The high ideals of France's policy of colonization and assimilation in Senegal were helped by the increasing presence of European women.

There were nearly 1,500 women by 1926 and they made a great impact on the domestic scene. There were a series of colonial handbooks dedicated to the problems of their activities and diversions. These included "Care of African Children" and "Studies of Flora and Fauna"! Evening-dress was compulsory on most social occasions!

When I visited Dakar in 1979 I found it a very impressive, beautiful city and a perfect holiday resort. President Léopold Sédar Senghor, whose encouragement of Black Culture and Art, which had a profound effect in raising the status of the Negro, is France's most famous modern Symbolist poet.

Chapter One

1899

Walking along the corridor, Kelda heard the sound of somebody crying.

She paused, listened, and realised it came from the room of Yvette de Villon.

She stood still, controlling an impulse to knock on the door and ask what the matter was.

She knew it was not her job to interfere in any way with the older girls. Mrs. Gladwin had made that very clear when she had promoted her from being little more than a servant, doing all the odd jobs that nobody else would do, to the position of assistant mistress.

"As you play the piano well," she had said in the hard voice in which she spoke to her inferiors, "you will supervise the practising of the younger girls, and you will also sit in the Class-Room when they are doing their homework. That will relieve the proper mistresses."

She paused as if she was thinking what else she could pile on Kelda's shoulders, then added:

"Of course, your duties as regards the laundry and the sewing and mending will continue as before, but you can look on this as a promotion and you should be suitably grateful."

1

"Thank you, Ma'am," Kelda said automatically.

Mrs. Gladwin's eyes rested on her critically.

"I consider that gown to be too tight in the bodice," she said. "It is almost indecent."

"I am afraid I have grown out of it," Kelda said apologetically.

"Then let it out!"

"I have done that already, Madam."

"Excuses, always excuses to spend money!" Mrs. Gladwin exclaimed. "You may go."

Kelda had left the Headmistress's Study feeling vibrations of disapproval following her, and it was with a sigh of relief that she reached the passage outside.

She knew Mrs. Gladwin disliked her although she found her useful, and she had wondered why, until one of the older girls had enlightened her.

"Keep out of the Dragon's way, Kelda!" she had warned. "She is on the war-path and you know that she takes it out on you because you are so pretty."

Kelda had been too surprised to reply, but that evening when she had at last been able to retire to the garret bedroom where she slept, she had looked into the small, discoloured mirror which hung on the wall over the chest-of-drawers.

"Am I really pretty?" she asked herself, and knew astonishingly that it was the truth.

She had come to Mrs. Gladwin's Seminary for Young Ladies when she was fifteen, from the Orphanage where she had lived for three years after her father and mother had been killed in an earthquake in Turkey.

Philip Lawrence had been an Archaeologist and the National Geographical Society had sent him to Turkey on a journey of exploration. It was a great concession that they had allowed him, because he had insisted, to take his wife with him.

There had been no question of their paying for anybody else, but somehow Philip Lawrence had scraped together the money to take his only child along as well.

It was nothing new for Kelda to accompany her father and mother on their travels and she had loved every moment of it.

Then her father and mother had been killed, and she had always bitterly regretted that on that particular day she had not been with them.

She had been very tired after a long expedition they had just taken, and they had left her behind in the cheap Boarding-House where they had stayed the night; since she was still asleep when they departed, they had not awakened her.

Often she would cry, not only because she had lost them but also because she had not said good-bye to the two people she loved most and who comprised her whole world.

After that she had never really known who had decided that she should go to an Orphanage on the outskirts of London.

She supposed it was one of the Missionaries who had taken charge of her, but she had been suffering from shock and nothing had seemed real until she found herself a "Charity Child" with fifty other orphans of varying ages, many of them having been in the Orphanage since the time they were born.

They accepted it philosophically because they had never known anything else; but to Kelda, who had been brought up with love and understanding, knowing the companionship of her father and the gentle sweetness of her mother, it had been like being plunged into the deepest hell with no chance of escape.

For three years she had suffered the almost intolerable humiliation of finding herself a nonentity, of being ordered about as if she had no feelings, of enduring bad food and little of it, and having to sleep with a dozen other children in a ward where they shivered miserably in the winter and panted with heat in the summer.

It had been an inexpressible relief when at fifteen she was told that she must start to earn her own living and was sent to Mrs. Gladwin's Seminary.

Here at least she heard cultured voices and ate what seemed good food, even though the pupils complained.

What was more important to Kelda than anything else was that she was now able to pick up her education again from where, on entering the Orphanage, she had been obliged to relinquish it.

Most of the children in the Orphanage could neither read nor write, and while a voluntary teacher came for two hours a day to teach them, there was no provision made for those who were more advanced or, like Kelda, extremely intelligent.

At the Seminary it was easy for her to take a lesson-book up to her bedroom at night, and although she was often too tired to absorb all she wished to do, over the years she had gradually become almost as knowledgeable as her father would have wished her to be.

The mistresses were constantly changing, but one or two of them were kind enough to lend her books of their own and sometimes even to explain to her things she did not understand.

There was a French mistress, an elderly woman to whom she carried secret cups of coffee after she had retired to bed, until she reciprocated by talking to her in French.

"You have a natural Parisian accent, my child," she said, "but you must practise your verbs. The English are always lazy over their verbs."

Kelda already spoke a certain amount of French, but she had been determined that she would be as fluent as her mother had been.

She therefore waited on *Mademoiselle* assiduously and was rewarded eventually by being told:

"Anyone who did not look at you would think that you were French. If they heard you speaking in the dark, they might easily be deceived."

It was a compliment which Kelda, who had never received any, treasured in her heart.

It had been a special delight to her when two years ago Yvette de Villon had come to the School.

She was French and came, Kelda discovered, from a family which was well known in France.

Kelda was not supposed to make friends with the girls but only to wait on them by pressing their gowns and mending anything that was beyond their own capabilities.

Kelda had managed by sheer persistence to ingratiate herself with the pretty French girl until Yvette confided in her and talked to her as an equal.

Even so, she was afraid to presume too much on their association, and she thought now that Yvette, who was often unpredictable, might resent it if she intruded on her grief.

What, Kelda asked herself, could have made Yvette cry?

She was not like some of the other girls who wept if one of the teachers was angry with them or who when they first arrived were desperately homesick.

Yvette was proud and in consequence had no particular "bosom friend" in the School to whom she turned in troubles, real or imaginary.

Her weeping, however, sounded so desperate that Kelda could bear it no longer.

She knocked very gently on the door and after a moment's silence Yvette asked in a quavering and hesitating voice:

"W-who . . . is it?"

Kelda turned the handle and, because she did not wish to be overheard, replied in a whisper:

"It is I, Kelda."

"Come in."

Kelda slipped into the room.

It was very small, as were all the rooms in the Seminary, but it had a personal look about it because Yvette had so many pretty things of her own in it.

There was an expensive lace cover on the narrow bedstead and a frilly satin cushion on the only chair. The wardrobe door was open and Kelda could see a profusion of gowns in bright colours, all of which had come from expensive Paris dressmakers.

But the face that was turned towards Kelda was very different from Yvette's usually attractive one.

Her eyes were swollen, her small nose was red, and tears were running down her cheeks.

"What is the matter?"

Kelda saw as she spoke that Yvette held a crumpled letter in one hand while the other clutched a handkerchief sodden with tears.

"Has something happened to somebody you love?" Kelda asked.

It was what she always suspected when she found that anybody was deeply unhappy, remembering how she herself had felt when her father and mother had died and there had been nobody to whom she could turn for comfort.

"No ... it is not ... that," Yvette answered.

Kelda knelt down beside her.

"Tell me what has upset you," she said. "Perhaps I can be of help."

"Nobody can ... help," Yvette replied, her voice breaking.

"Please tell me," Kelda begged.

"I have had a—letter, a letter from my—uncle."

"And it has upset you?"

"I hate him! I have always hated him, and now I have to go and—live with him!"

Kelda remembered that like herself Yvette was an orphan. Nevertheless, she had a great number of relations in France.

Every holiday when she returned to Paris she stayed with aunts and uncles who all had impressive-sounding titles and, Kelda discovered, romantic *Châteaux* on the Loire and Villas in the South.

Yvette returned to School with stories of the exciting times she had had, how many parties she had attended, and it seemed strange now that she should be thrown into such despondency.

Aloud Kelda said:

"I did not know you hated any of your relatives. With which uncle are you to stay?"

"My English uncle," Yvette answered. "He is horrible and if I live with him I shall never see France again, and—all my—friends."

She burst into tears again and Kelda rose to fetch her a fresh handkerchief from the chest-of-drawers.

She put it into Yvette's hand, then as the French girl mopped her eyes, she said:

"I had no idea you had an English uncle. You have never spoken of him."

"Why should I? I tell you . . . I hate him, but my aunt married him."

"And he lives in England?" Kelda asked. "Well, that will not be too bad. After all, you have many friends who are English here at the School."

"He does not live in England," Yvette replied, "but in Senegal."

It took Kelda a second or two to remember where Senegal was, then she thought she must be mistaken.

"You cannot mean Senegal in West Africa?"

Yvette nodded.

"My uncle lives there because he—dislikes Society. He is a recluse—an eccentric. Why should I have to—live with somebody like—that?"

Her voice sounded desperate.

"Is there any . . . reason why you should . . . obey him?" Kelda asked hesitatingly.

"Mama and Papa made him my Guardian a long time before they died," Yvette replied.

She paused for a moment to mop her eyes before she went on:

"Aunt Ginette was alive then, and as she was Mama's younger sister I suppose they thought that if anything should happen to them, Aunt Ginette would take Mama's place. But she is dead, and that leaves Uncle Maximus, whom I have always—hated and who I am sure hates—me."

"If that is true, why would he want you to come live with him?" Kelda asked practically.

"I expect he wants to imprison me in Africa, where I can never see anybody of whom I am fond, and have no parties or enjoy anything that will amuse me, and just become—old and—embittered as he is."

"How do you know he is like that?" Kelda asked.

"I saw him five years ago," Yvette answered, "and some of my other relatives have seen him since and say he has grown even worse than he was then."

Kelda could think of no reply to this and after a moment Yvette went on:

"There is some mystery about him which makes them always stop talking when I come into the room, but I have often heard my cousins say laughingly that I have too much money and might become cynical like Uncle Maximus."

"He is rich then," Kelda said. "Perhaps he wants to leave you all his money."

"I do not want his money," Yvette retorted. "I have plenty of my own. Papa and Mama left me everything they had. I may not spend it until I am twenty-one, and that is more than three years ahead! Three years in which I shall have to live with Uncle Maximus and ask him for every penny I require."

She burst into such a flood of tears that Kelda could only put her arms round her and hold her close.

"It may not be as bad as you think," she said soothingly, "and it will be interesting for you to see Senegal."

She remembered now her father talking to her about West Africa and saying he would like to go there.

Kelda had been with him once to Algeria, but that had been a long time ago, and it was difficult to remember very much about it, except that it had been full of sunshine and she and her father and mother had found a lot that amused them.

They had stayed for a short time in Algiers and had found the city fascinating.

"I will look up the geography-books about Senegal," she said, "and tell you all about it. Where does your uncle live?"

"I do not care where he lives," Yvette said petulantly. "It will be beastly, like him, and I shall loathe every moment of it!"

"It might be better than you think," Kelda said. "Tell me where he lives."

"You can see the address for yourself," Yvette replied, and flung the letter she held in her hand onto the floor.

Kelda bent down and picked it up.

She realised that both the envelope and the writing-paper were of the thickest and most expensive quality and both bore an impressive crest.

She did not like to make Yvette think she was prying by reading the letter, but as she looked at the address, noting that it was in Dakar, her eye also caught the first line on the writing-paper, written in a strong, upright hand.

My dear Niece . . . she read.

It struck her as being an unnecessarily formal manner of addressing Yvette, but aloud she said:

"I am sure there will be a great deal in the books about Dakar, and I am also certain that it is under French administration. So there will be French people living there and you will not feel so lonely as you anticipate."

"I want to stay in France," Yvette insisted. "I want to be in Paris, where I can dance and go to all the lovely Balls that are to be given for me when I leave the School at Christmas."

Kelda had thought it likely that as Yvette would be eighteen at the beginning of next year, she would leave Mrs. Gladwin's either at Christmas or at Easter.

Because she was fond of the French girl she had known that she would miss her, and at the moment there was no other pupil to take her place in her affections.

"I do not know what I shall do without you," she said with a deep sigh.

"If I asked if I could stay here for another six months," Yvette said suddenly, "do you think they would let me?"

Kelda looked down at the letter she still held in her hand.

Somehow, she did not quite know why, she felt as if there were vibrations of power coming from it and an unmistakable aura of authority.

"I think if your Guardian says you are to leave, then you will have to do so," she said quietly.

Yvette sprang to her feet.

"Why should I live with someone I hate?" she asked. "Why should he order me about, not even asking me if there is anything else I would prefer to do?"

She paused for a moment before she said angrily:

"I presume you know the answer to that. I would rather live in a garret in Paris than in a Palace in Dakar!"

"Is that what he owns?" Kelda asked curiously.

"I imagine that is what it will be," Yvette replied. "As he is so rich and pompous, he obviously lords it over the wretched natives!"

Kelda put the letter down on the table, resisting an impulse to ask Yvette if she could read it.

'There is nothing I can do to help her,' she thought sadly.

She was just about to say how sorry she was when there was a knock on the door which made both the girls start.

"Who is it?" Yvette enquired.

"Madam wants to see you in her Study, M'mselle," one of the maids replied.

She went away without waiting for an answer and they heard her heavy footsteps going down the passage.

Yvette looked at Kelda.

"The Dragon will have received a letter too, and I bet she is drooling over it because Uncle Maximus has a title!"

Mrs. Gladwin was a snob who fawned upon all the parents whose names appeared in Debrett, and it was a joke which never ceased to amuse her pupils.

Yvette was not smiling now. Instead she said:

"You can be sure that the Dragon will make me do exactly what Uncle Maximus wants."

"You had better go downstairs and find out what she has to say," Kelda said, "but you should wash your face first."

"Let her see it as it is," Yvette replied. "I shall try to persuade her to write to my French relatives and protest at my being sent off to some outlandish place, although I doubt if she will do so."

"I think it very unlikely," Kelda agreed, "and even if they do protest, they will not have any authority under the law."

"Uncle Maximus has not taken the slightest interest in me until now," Yvette said. "He has not written to me at Christmas or even sent me a card. Why should he want me to live with him? Why this sudden interest?"

"It does seem strange," Kelda agreed. "Perhaps he feels lonely."

"Lonely? Uncle Maximus? According to Cousin Jacques, recluse though he may be, he always has a mistress."

Kelda looked shocked.

"I cannot believe your cousin told you that!"

"Not exactly," Yvette admitted, "but he visited Uncle Maximus when he was on his way to Cape

Town, and he told his brother, when he did not
know I was listening, that when he called on him
he had a glimpse of a beautiful woman. 'Mind you,'
he added, 'I have a suspicion she was a *métisse.*'"

Yvette wrinkled her brow.

"What is a *métisse?* I asked Aunt Jeanne-Marie,
but she would not tell me."

Kelda knew it meant the offspring of the white
company-employees and local women, but she was
not going to explain that to Yvette.

Instead she replied:

"I will look it up in the dictionary and let you
know."

"I have done that already," Yvette said, "but
it was not there, unless I got the spelling wrong."

"You must hurry to Madam," Kelda insisted. "You
know how cross she gets if one keeps her waiting."

"Why should I care, if I am leaving?" Yvette
replied.

Kelda was tidying her hair, then she found her
another handkerchief.

"I will wash these," she said, picking up the two
tear-stained ones. "Is there anything else I can do for
you?"

"Nothing," Yvette replied, "unless you can cast a
spell on Uncle Maximus so that he will fall dead!"

She walked across the room and as she reached
the door she stopped.

"That is quite an idea!" she said. "I believe
there is lots of Black Magic in Africa. I shall try to
find a Witch Doctor as soon as I get there and see
if he can dispose of my uncle for me."

Kelda gave a little cry of horror.

"That is a wicked thing to say! I know you will
do nothing of the sort!"

"Do not be too sure of that!" Yvette answered
sharply as she flounced away down the passage.

Kelda sighed and automatically began to tidy
the room.

She was sorry for Yvette. At the same time, she

wished she had the opportunity of travelling to Senegal or anywhere else in the world, as she had done when her father was alive.

She knew now that the one thing that had been harder to bear than anything else was the feeling of being restricted and restrained first by the drab, dark walls of the Orphanage, then by the Seminary.

When her father and mother were alive they had never stayed for long in any one place.

Even if Philip Lawrence had not been sent on some important expedition, he had travelled about England giving lectures at various Universities and Kelda could remember twice going to Edinburgh.

Their journeys had seldom been very comfortable, but it had been an excitement to be on the move.

More than anything else it had been a thrill to be in a foreign country, to ride on the back of a camel or a stubborn mule, to sail in a small boat with a big sail up some river to places which could not be reached by any other means.

"Oh, Papa, I miss you," Kelda said beneath her breath.

She knew that the eight years since he had died were a nightmare from which she half-believed she might still wake.

To look back made her remember that while Yvette was not quite eighteen and was going out into the world for the first time, she would be twenty-one in July. She supposed her life would never alter from what it was at the moment.

She often wondered if she left the Seminary whether she would be able to find other employment of a more congenial nature.

Although she had often considered it, she thought it was unlikely, and in a way she clung to Mrs. Gladwin because with her she was with girls who came from cultured families.

It was not that they or Mrs. Gladwin considered her their equal. The latter continually reminded her that she came from an Orphanage and was nothing but a "Charity Child."

At first Kelda had resented it, feeling that she must reply that her father was a gentleman and her mother a lady, even if they had had no money.

Then she decided that such retorts only made the situation more difficult than it was at the moment.

Mrs. Gladwin liked humiliating her because, unlike the servants, she could not leave, nor would she answer back as the Governesses could do.

She therefore taught herself to control her feelings, to try not to listen when Mrs. Gladwin found fault incessantly and expected her to be eternally grateful for having a roof over her head and food to eat.

She was certainly paid little enough for her services—a quarter of what any of the servants received—but she knew that if she was dissatisfied there was nothing she could do about it.

Even these meagre wages were overdue, and because Kelda loathed having to ask for what she was owed since doing so precipitated a lecture on how grateful she should be for being where she was, she had not even mentioned the fact to her employer.

She crossed the room to shut the wardrobe door, and as she did so she looked at the gowns hanging inside it, many of which Yvette had worn only two or three times.

Kelda remembered how pretty her mother had always looked, despite the fact that she could never afford anything expensive.

"It is not only what you spend," she had said once, "it is having good taste and knowing what suits oneself."

'Perhaps if I had the chance,' Kelda thought, 'I too would have good taste.'

She had only to look in the mirror to realise that the grey gown she wore, which was made of the coarsest cotton, was unbecoming and looked, as indeed she was, poverty-stricken.

It had of course been chosen by Mrs. Gladwin, who, ever since Kelda had come to the Seminary, had insisted on repeating the same grey garments she had worn in the Orphanage rather than buying her dresses of a brighter and more cheerful colour.

"Please, Madam," she had asked a year ago, "as I am having a new gown, could it be in blue or green?"

"I consider both those colours quite unsuitable for your position," Mrs. Gladwin replied acidly. "What is more, they would show the dirt."

"I wash my gowns every week," Kelda said quickly.

"I should have thought that was unnecessarily often," Mrs. Gladwin replied, determined to find fault. "The uniform I choose for you is what I permit you to wear, and there will be no arguments about it."

She was dismissed, and as she left the Study Kelda knew it had been a forlorn hope anyway that she might be allowed to look more attractive.

Now as she shut the wardrobe door she thought of what she would buy if she could afford it. She was sure blue and pale green would be becoming to her as they had been to her mother.

She had the same fair golden hair, the same large blue-grey eyes that were the colour of the morning mist, and her skin was transparently clear, although she was pale and too thin from overwork.

She caught a glimpse of herself in the mirror and turned away from it.

What was the point of pretending? She would wear grey and the years ahead would be grey too.

If only Yvette knew how very lucky she was to be able to escape to Senegal or anywhere else in the world!

There were innumerable duties which kept Kelda busy until supper-time.

One of the jobs which had been thought up for her by Mrs. Gladwin was that she should wait on the mistresses who had supper in their own rooms.

They took it in turns to supervise the pupils in the large Dining-Room where everybody had to eat at luncheon-time.

The mistresses themselves insisted that in the evening, those who were not on duty should be served in their own Sitting-Rooms, where they could add to the School-fare delicacies which had been purchased either by themselves or sent to them by relatives.

At first Mrs. Gladwin had resisted such an innovation. Then when she found there were no reasonable arguments she could use against it, she assuaged her pride by saying that the servants were too busy but that Kelda could wait on the mistresses, bringing their meals in from the kitchen and washing up afterwards.

Kelda had not really minded, for as a result she often enjoyed tid-bits that the mistresses left, which was a change from the School meals which repeated themselves in monotonous rotation from week to week with no variation.

Tonight when she entered the Staff-Room it was to find an animated conversation taking place.

"I said to her," Miss Dawson, one of the older mistresses, was declaiming, " 'I have no intention, Madam, of spending my holiday by travelling to some outlandish part of the world. I dislike the sea and always have, and I have no plans for ever leaving these shores again!' "

There was a burst of laughter as Kelda put the heavy tray down on a side-table.

"What did she say to that?"

"She merely dismissed me and sent for Miss Jenkins."

"Did you accept her proposition?" someone asked. "Tell us, Jenky. We are all ears!"

"Of course I did not," Miss Jenkins, who was

the Games Mistress, replied. "I'm spending my holiday with my fiancé at his home. I would not give that up for a trip to Heaven and back again!"

Again there was laughter as Kelda ladeled out the soup and set it down on the table in front of each of the mistresses.

"Who did she try next?" someone questioned.

"I think she has been through the lot of us," Miss Dawson said. "I know Ashton told me before she went out this evening that she had refused, and I think Miss Hart has said no."

"Madam is so keen on pleasing this nobleman," Miss Jenkins said, "that I cannot think why she does not go herself, or alternatively she could send Kelda."

Kelda started at the sound of her own name and they all laughed.

"As a matter of fact," Miss Jenkins said, "I actually suggested that."

"You didn't!" Miss Dawson exclaimed. "You must have been feeling cheeky. We all know what she thinks of Kelda."

"She was furious! That is why I said it," Miss Jenkins replied, laughing. "She knows we are all aware that Kelda is the only person in this place whom she can treat in that high-handed manner, as if she were the Panjandrum himself. None of us would stick it!"

"That is true," Miss Jenkins said. "I have often wondered, Kelda, why you don't leave."

Kelda was bringing the last bowl of soup to the table and she smiled.

"The answer to that is simple," she said. "It is because I have nowhere else to go."

"And no money either, I suppose," Miss Jenkins said.

"I have not been paid for six months," Kelda replied, "and if I was, I doubt if it would get me farther than Piccadilly Circus."

They all laughed as if she had said something very funny.

"I think it's a crying shame," Miss Jenkins said. "But never mind—perhaps one day a rich uncle you've forgotten about will turn up and carry you off to Timbuctoo. One never knows one's luck!"

"I can always go on hoping," Kelda answered.

She picked up the tray and went out of the room. As she shut the door behind her she heard Miss Dawson say:

"It is a disgrace the way Madam treats that nice girl."

"That is what I think," Miss Ashton said, "but there is nothing we can do about it and I suppose as a 'Charity Child' she is lucky to be here."

Kelda did not wait to hear any more. She hurried down towards the kitchen, feeling as if her feet echoed the same words:

"Charity Child!" "Charity Child!"

She felt as if they were branded on her and she would never be anything else however hard she tried! A "Charity Child" everyone could trample on and for whom there was little hope now or in the future!

* * *

When she had finished washing up the mistresses' supper, Kelda made a cup of cocoa and carried it upstairs to Yvette.

It was strictly against the rules, but she thought it might help the French girl to sleep, knowing that her unhappiness would doubtless keep her tossing and turning all through the night.

She opened the door to find that Yvette was already undressed, sitting in front of the mirror with a sulky expression on her face.

"I have brought you some cocoa," Kelda said.

"That is kind of you, Kelda," Yvette replied. "I could not eat any supper. I was too unhappy."

"Are you hungry? Shall I go downstairs and get you a sandwich?"

"No, I do not want anything to eat, but I will enjoy the cocoa. Did you put plenty of sugar in it?"

"Three teaspoonfuls," Kelda answered. " 'Hot and sweet' was what my mother always prescribed when somebody had had a shock."

"It is certainly what I have had."

"What did Madam say to you?"

"Only what you know already: that I have to go and live with Uncle Maximus. He has instructed her to send me to him, as if I were a parcel, accompanied by one of the mistresses from the School to see that I reach him without mishap."

"The mistresses have all refused to go."

"I know that," Yvette said. "Madam called me into the Study after prayers to ask: 'Have you any relations in England who would accompany you to Dakar?'

" 'No, Madam,' I replied, 'and if I had, they would not take me. They all dislike my uncle as much as I do.' "

Kelda gave a little laugh.

"I am sure Madam was shocked at your speaking like that."

"Horrified!" Yvette agreed. "She looked down that long nose of hers and said:

" 'That is not the way to speak of your uncle, Yvette. I am sure what he is doing is in your best interests.'

" 'My best interests, Madam,' I replied, 'would be to live in France with the relations I love and who love me. I have no wish to go to Senegal, and I have a very good mind to run away'!"

Kelda laughed and it was a sound of pure enjoyment.

"How brave of you! I do not know how you dared to speak to her like that."

Yvette shrugged her shoulders in a typically French gesture.

"She can do nothing to me now that is any worse than what Uncle Maximus is doing."

"What did she say?"

"She gave me a long lecture on propriety and how I should not only damage myself but also the reputation of the School by speaking in such a 'pert and unladylike fashion.'"

Yvette deliberately imitated Mrs. Gladwin's voice as she said the last phrase, and both she and Kelda laughed again.

"What did she say after that?" Kelda asked.

"She went on until she ran out of breath," Yvette replied. "Then I said: 'I am not surprised that none of the mistresses will accompany me to Senegal, and I certainly have no wish to be buried alive there myself. If it is impossible for you to find anybody to accompany me, perhaps you could tell my uncle it would be best for me to stay here. Or, alternatively, let Kelda come with me. She, at least, as an explorer's daughter, will not object to travelling in darkest Africa.'"

Kelda gave a gasp.

"That is what Miss Jenkins suggested. What did Madam reply?"

"I did not wait to hear," Yvette answered. "I went out of the room while she was still gasping for breath like a gold-fish that has been left out of water!"

"She must have been furious!" Kelda said.

There was a note in her voice which made Yvette say quickly:

"Oh, Kelda, I hope I did not make her so angry that she takes it out on you."

"So do I," Kelda said.

She felt apprehensive, thinking that if two people had made the same suggestion it would doubtless infuriate Madam to the point where she would think of some very unpleasant punishment for her.

She changed the subject, as it made her feel rather nervous, and asked:

"When do you go?"

"Two days before the end of term. Madam would

not let me leave if Uncle Maximus had not insisted that I should travel in some specific ship which stops at Dakar on its way to the Cape."

"It sounds very exciting!" Kelda said.

"You know how I feel about it," Yvette said in a forlorn voice. "I do wish you could come with me. At least there would be someone human to talk to. If old Dawson had accepted Madam's proposal I think I should have died! You know what a bore she is at any time."

"I would love to come with you," Kelda said, "but you know as well as I do that it would be like asking for the moon."

"I suppose so," Yvette said despairingly. "But you say all the mistresses have refused."

"They all said they had at supper," Kelda replied, "including Miss Ashton, who is not in tonight."

"Then who will the Dragon send with me?" Yvette asked.

"I have no idea. Perhaps she has a friend who would like to journey to Africa, or perhaps she will go herself!"

"Then I shall definitely jump overboard!" Yvette said firmly. "I am not travelling with old Gladwin, and that's a fact!"

Even as she spoke, the door opened and to Yvette's and Kelda's astonishment Mrs. Gladwin came into the room.

It was very unsual for her to leave her own quarters once supper was over, and she seldom visited the girls' bedrooms except during her inspections which took place once a week in the morning.

Then she would walk round deliberately to find fault, and it was Kelda's self-appointed task to hide away anything the girls had forgotten which she thought might evoke Mrs. Gladwin's disapproval before she appeared.

Food, fruit, and sweets were forbidden, and anything decorative or in any way ostentatious was always in danger of being confiscated.

As Mrs. Gladwin now stepped into the room, it was so unexpected and in a way so unusual that for several perceptible seconds Yvette forgot to rise from her chair.

Mrs. Gladwin, however, was glaring at Kelda.

"I had a suspicion I might find you here, Kelda," she said. "As I have told you before, I will not have you gossiping in the young ladies' rooms, which is neither proper nor in the sphere of your duties. If you have nothing better to do, I will certainly find you something."

"As *Mademoiselle* was so upset today," Kelda said in her soft voice, "I brought her something warm to drink, knowing that it was in a way a medication."

"If Yvette needs one I will send for the Physician," Mrs. Gladwin said automatically.

She then looked sharply at Yvette.

"I presume," she said, "you have been crying again and making a quite unnecessary fuss about your uncle's plans for your future."

As she was already so over-wrought, the tears gathered in Yvette's eyes, and Mrs. Gladwin went on:

"You must learn to control yourself. As I have told you so often, self-control comes from being civilised and properly educated."

Yvette did not reply, and as she was searching for her handkerchief in the belt of her gown two tears rolled down her cheeks.

"I have been thinking over the difficulties of your reaching Dakar," Mrs. Gladwin said. "That is why I have come to ask you once again if there is anybody you know in England who would be prepared to accompany you on this journey."

"I have already told you, Madam, I know of no-one," Yvette said.

"There is no Governess you have had in the past who would be prepared, for a remuneration, a small one of course, to act as your Chaperone?"

"The Governess I had before I came here," Yvette

replied, "has a position in Paris teaching the children of the *Duc* de Beauclaire. So I am quite certain she would be unable to come with me, even if she wanted to, which I very much doubt."

Mrs. Gladwin ignored the last words, which were obviously rude, and stood thinking in the centre of the small bedroom.

Kelda would have liked to inch past her and reach the door, but she had a feeling it would only bring more wrath down upon her head.

She therefore stood where she was, hoping she could fade into the background and not draw any unnecessary attention to herself.

"Very well," Mrs. Gladwin said at last, as if she had just made up her mind, "if that is actually the position, the only thing I can do is send Kelda with you."

She paused for a moment, ignoring the startled expressions on both Yvette's and Kelda's faces, and went on:

"Of course, being a 'Charity Child' she is nothing more than a servant, and she can act in the capacity of your lady's-maid as well as keeping you constantly in her sight."

There was still no response from either of the two girls to whom she was speaking, and she went on as if to herself:

"I shall naturally send a letter immediately to the steam-ship company explaining your circumstances, and I am quite certain your uncle's name will carry great weight with them, so there will be no difficulty about your having the best possible attention."

She paused before she continued:

"I shall also ask if there are any respectable English people on board. The steam-ship authorities will, I believe, as they do in the case of ladies travelling to India, invite one of the lady passengers to keep an eye on you and in fact act as your official Chaperone until you reach Dakar."

Yvette found her voice.

"I shall be . . . all right with . . . Kelda."

"That is what I hope, although I am none too confident of her capabilities in looking after herself, let alone you," Mrs. Gladwin retorted. "But I am certain, yes, I am quite certain that there will be someone on board to whom you can be entrusted once the ship has left Southampton. I shall in fact take you on board myself so that your uncle will have no reason to worry about you."

Mrs. Gladwin stopped speaking to look at Kelda's wide eyes and pale face.

"As for you, Kelda," she said, "if you fail the charge I have put upon you, if you are unworthy of my trust, I can assure you that you will never darken the doors of this house again!"

Mrs. Gladwin did not wait for a reply, but merely turned with a rustling of her silk petticoats.

"Go to bed, Yvette," she said, "and say a prayer of gratitude to God that you have somebody like myself to take care of you, who has your interests at heart."

Mrs. Gladwin left the room.

For a moment neither Yvette nor Kelda moved.

It was almost as if they had been turned into stone.

Then Kelda, beneath her breath and in a voice that was barely above a whisper, said:

"It is not . . . true! I could not have . . . heard what she . . . said! I must be . . . dreaming!"

"It is true," Yvette answered, "although I can hardly believe it! And, Kelda, if anything could make the journey to my uncle bearable, it is knowing that you are coming with me. I shall say a prayer of gratitude all right, but only because without you I know I should die of misery on the voyage!"

Chapter Two

As the steam-ship moved out of Southampton Harbour and down into the English Channel, Kelda had gripped her fingers together to make sure she was not dreaming.

She could hardly believe it was possible that for the moment at any rate, she was leaving behind the misery she had felt at the Seminary, and England itself, where for the last eight years she had been consistently unhappy to the point of despair.

Now like the wave of a magic wand everything was changed.

At least for two months she would be free of Mrs. Gladwin's fault-finding and of continually being reminded that she was nothing but a "Charity Child."

It had been a thrill for her, although not for Yvette, that she was on board a ship.

Because Lord Orsett was obviously very rich and important, they were allotted two of the best cabins on the First Class deck which communicated with each other.

There were a large number of obliging stewards to carry their luggage and to ask if there was anything they could do to serve them.

Kelda's luggage certainly looked pathetically small beside the enormous amount of trunks in which she had packed Yvette's gowns, bonnets, sunshades, and a number of things she had insisted on buying at the last moment.

"If I have to go to some benighted hole at the other end of the world," she had said defiantly to Mrs. Gladwin, "I am not going to be ashamed of my appearance, and so until I actually leave I intend to spend the time shopping."

For once Mrs. Gladwin had no viable arguments as to why she should not do so. Because the mistresses could not be spared, Kelda had accompanied Yvette on a number of shopping-expeditions for which a closed carriage was hired, as of course Yvette was not allowed to travel by public transport.

It was all so exciting that Kelda had found herself praying at night that nothing would happen to prevent her from going to Senegal, even though she knew that as every day their departure drew nearer, Yvette became more despondent.

"I shall be buried—buried alive," she kept saying over and over again, and there was nothing Kelda could say to console her.

She wrote to all her relatives in Paris, begging them to intervene on her behalf, but they wrote back saying that there was nothing they could do as her uncle was her Guardian.

Kelda, who saw the letters, had a feeling that they were in fact over-awed by Lord Orsett's wealth and importance.

"Why did he go to Senegal in the first place?" she had asked.

Yvette shrugged her shoulders.

"I cannot imagine, unless it was to be different from everyone else."

"Had he been there before he married your aunt?"

"I do not think so. I have always heard that Aunt Ginette was very pretty and enjoyed gaiety and parties."

"It seems strange that he should have taken her to Africa."

"Everything about Uncle Maximus is strange," Yvette said, "and I cannot understand why Mama ever made him my Guardian."

"I suppose she thought he would look after you properly and could afford to do so," Kelda replied.

"You keep talking about his money," Yvette said sharply. "Have you forgotten that I am an heiress?"

"Only now that your father and mother are dead," Kelda said gently.

Yvette did not reply, because she hated to talk about her uncle, and Kelda knew that she was becoming increasingly apprehensive about seeing him again.

There were so many questions she wanted to ask, but as she knew they would upset Yvette, she thought it best to wait until they had actually begun their journey towards her mysterious relative to live in a part of Africa which seemed mysterious too.

Kelda had searched every guide-book in the School to find out something about Senegal, but although it had been officially a French Colony since 1848, there was very little written about it in the history-books which were predominately English.

The geography-books contented themselves with merely showing a map of the area and reiterating that it was under the French.

She discovered, however, that four years earlier a decree had created the Government-General of French West Africa, headed by a Governor-General.

She found that Senegal had the equivalent of the Council of a French Department, but she was not quite certain what this meant.

She longed to have somebody to explain all these matters to her before she actually arrived in Senegal, and she thought that this was perhaps where she missed her father's wisdom and knowledge of the world more than she had ever missed him before.

"How thrilled Papa would be to think I was going off exploring again," she told herself, then wondered desperately how long her expedition would last.

Mrs. Gladwin had been quite firm that she was to return to England as soon as Yvette had settled down with her uncle.

"Get it firmly into your head, Kelda," she had said in her disagreeable voice, "that you are only going as a travelling companion with *Mademoiselle* since I cannot find anyone else. You will not intrude in any way upon His Lordship's household, and you will return at the first possible opportunity."

She paused and added almost spitefully:

"I shall expect you back in January without fail."

Kelda nodded her head in agreement because there was nothing else she could do.

But she knew that once Mrs. Gladwin had left the ship in which they were to travel, she would pray every night that she would never see her again and would find some excuse for staying in Dakar, or any other part of the world where she could earn her living in a different way.

"Perhaps there will be Schools in which I can teach, or I might even serve in a shop," she told herself.

Then she laughed as she remembered the native bazaars and markets she had attended with her father and mother, and knew that the idea of a white woman being employed in them was very impractical if not impossible.

For the moment, however, she was in a ship travelling from one port to another and therefore in a "no-man's-land" where she was free of any restrictions except those imposed upon her by her own sense of propriety.

Mrs. Gladwin had, of course, written to the steam-ship company seeking a Chaperone for Yvette.

The Purser had introduced her to an elderly couple, a Methodist Minister and his wife, who were returning to South Africa after a visit to England to see their children.

As they had very little money of their own, they were deeply grateful that their congregation had contrived to raise the money for their fares and had insisted, because they were both elderly, that they travel First Class.

They had been overwhelmed when Mrs. Gladwin bore down upon them like a ship at full sail and they had hastily agreed to everything she had asked.

Kelda had realised they were far too retiring and unassuming to think of interfering with anyone, least of all with somebody as pretty and obviously aristocratic as Yvette.

Because they took Kelda in her drab garments to be little more than a senior servant, they could talk to her more easily, but after two days at sea they both felt unwell and she found herself looking after them rather than they after Yvette and herself.

The first night aboard, Yvette began to take an interest in the other passengers.

"A rather dull lot, I think," she said to Kelda, "with the exception of one young man who looks interesting."

"Where is he?" Kelda asked.

It had been announced the first night at sea that passengers could sit anywhere they wished and that their proper places at the Captain's and the Chief Officers' tables would be allotted the following day.

Kelda had travelled enough to know that this was a precaution on the part of the Captain against overlooking any important passenger who by rights should have been sitting at his table, only to find later that there was no place for him.

She thought it wise to ask the Chief Steward when they entered the Dining-Saloon if she and Yvette could have one of the small tables for two.

"Why have you asked for this table?" Yvette enquired as soon as they were seated.

"It will give us a chance to look round," Kelda explained, "and know who to avoid."

Yvette laughed.

"I never thought of that, but I can see quite a number of people who will come into that category."

"My father used to laugh about ships' bores who told the same story over and over again from Portsmouth to Port Said, and Mama used to run away from the gossips who disparaged anyone who was in the least attractive and said the most slanderous things about them."

Yvette laughed again.

"That will be me!"

"In which case, please be careful," Kelda begged. "Do not forget I am in charge of you, and if you behave badly I shall get the blame."

"Who is to know how I behave?" Yvette asked. "Besides, if I have an outrageous reputation by the time I arrive at Dakar, perhaps Uncle Maximus will send me home to Paris in disgrace."

"I would not bank on it," Kelda replied, "but please, dearest Yvette, remember how angry he will be with me and that I shall be sent back, not to Paris like you, but to Mrs. Gladwin."

Yvette made a grimace.

"We must certainly stop that from happening," she said. "And I have every intention, Kelda, of keeping you with me whatever Uncle Maximus may say."

This statement did not make Kelda feel as happy as it should have.

From all she had heard about Lord Orsett, she was quite certain that he would do exactly what he wanted to do and would make everyone else do the same.

If he wished her to leave she would leave, whatever Yvette might say in the matter, but she went on praying that someone, somehow, would save her from returning to England.

Yvette had noticed a rather good-looking young

man the first night, and when she pointed him out, Kelda saw that he had noticed her.

It might have been chance, but Kelda suspected it was connivance, when after they had been allotted places at the Captain's table for luncheon the following day, the young man was seated next to Yvette.

They learnt that his name was Rémy Mendès, but at luncheon they only exchanged commonplace remarks on the weather, the speed of the ship, and the fact that as there were so few young people on board it looked as if it would be difficult to arrange sports of any kind.

"I shall have to get my exercise by jogging round the deck," *Monsieur* Mendès said, "but I would much rather play badminton or quoits, although I believe the latter is rather hard on the hands."

"I can play badminton," Yvette said, "although not very well, I am afraid."

"Then I must certainly challenge you to a game," *Monsieur* Mendès replied instantly, as she had obviously intended him to do.

As soon as luncheon was over Yvette and Kelda went into the Saloon as it was too rough and too cold for them to go outside on deck.

Kelda was not surprised that they had no sooner seated themselves in a corner of the room and ordered coffee than *Monsieur* Mendès asked if he could join them.

Yvette introduced Kelda, and it was obvious that after one glance at her clothes, he thought she was merely a paid Chaperone, and after a formal bow he concentrated entirely on Yvette.

"Now we can talk," he said in a manner that was obviously intended only for her ears.

His dark eyes looked into Yvette's and there was no doubt about the look of admiration in them or the fact that he was already very attracted to her.

"I wonder if I ought to do anything about it," Kelda asked herself, and had no idea what the answer should be.

"Are you going to Cape Town?" he asked. "I believe it is a very attractive place, although I have never been there."

"No, I am going to Dakar," Yvette replied.

"To Dakar?"

There was no doubt that *Monsieur* Mendès was astonished.

Yvette did not reply and he said:

"I cannot believe it! Did you really say Dakar?"

"I have to go there to stay with my uncle," Yvette explained, "but I assure you I would much rather be going on to Cape Town."

Kelda thought it was rather indiscreet of her to tell her troubles so quickly to a stranger.

But *Monsieur* Mendès cried:

"I would much rather you came to Dakar, because that is where I am going! But I can hardly believe that anyone as lovely as you would set foot in such a benighted place."

"Do you live in Dakar?" Yvette enquired.

"Only temporarily, thank God!" he replied. "I am, as it happens, for the next three months Diplomatic Equerry to the Governor-General."

Yvette clasped her hands together.

"But that is wonderful! I shall see you!"

"You can be sure of that," he said. "Who is your uncle?"

"Lord Orsett."

Again the astonishment on *Monsieur* Mendès's face was very apparent.

"Lord Orsett? But he never has visitors, and I certainly never suspected that he had a niece who looks like you."

"Tell me about Dakar," Yvette suggested. "As you can imagine, I have no wish to go there when I might be in Paris."

"I can understand that," *Monsieur* Mendès said. "I too miss Paris, but thank goodness I shall be back there in time for the Spring."

"There will be chestnut-trees blossoming in the Champs Élysées," Yvette said wistfully.

"And flowers in the Bois!"   -

"There will be Balls and parties," Yvette continued in a rapt voice, "and I had planned how I would dance until dawn."

"That is exactly what you should do," *Monsieur* Mendès said. "But how is it possible that you are travelling to Dakar?"

"Lord Orsett is my uncle by marriage and also my Guardian."

"I remember hearing that he had had a French wife," *Monsieur* Mendès said. "I suppose that is why he came to live in Dakar originally, but she must have hated it as much as you will."

"What shall I do?" Yvette asked. "Tell me what I shall do."

"I promise you one thing," he said. "I will do everything in my power to make your stay in Dakar as pleasant as possible."

"But you will be going away."

"Not until the middle of March, and a lot may happen before then."

The way he spoke made Yvette feel shy and she looked down so that her eye-lashes were dark against her pale skin.

'She is very pretty,' Kelda thought to herself. 'It is not surprising that he cannot take his eyes from her face.'

She wondered at the same time what Lord Orsett would say if they arrived in Dakar accompanied by a young man.

It was quite obvious from that moment that *Monsieur* Mendès was bowled over by Yvette and she by him.

"He is charming, delightful, intelligent!" Yvette said when she and Kelda were undressing the first night, and on the second night she said with a dreamy look in her eyes:

"I think, Kelda, I am falling in love!"

"Please, Yvette, please be careful!" Kelda begged. "I am sure it is unwise to be precipitate in such matters. We know nothing about *Monsieur* Mendès. Your uncle may not approve of him."

"I am quite sure Uncle Maximus approves only of himself!" Yvette said with a scowl. "But I will find out everything you want to know. *Monsieur* Mendès has asked me to meet him on the top deck tomorrow morning, and if it is not raining we can sit somewhere sheltered and talk without being watched by all those old pussy-cats who were staring at us at dinner tonight."

It was obvious, Kelda thought, why the elderly women at the Captain's table had looked with raised eye-brows at the manner in which Yvette and *Monsieur* Mendès were engrossed with each other all through the meal.

He made no effort to speak to the lady on his other side, and as Yvette had Kelda next to her, she saw no point in dividing her attention.

Kelda had therefore been left to talk to an elderly trader who she learnt often visited Senegal to buy ground-nuts, which were, he informed her, their only appreciable export at the moment.

He was partly deaf, and although Kelda would have liked to ask him about Senegal she found it somewhat embarrassing when she had to shout every question several times before he understood her.

After dinner, to Kelda's consternation, Yvette and *Monsieur* Mendès suddenly disappeared.

She could not ask anyone if they had seen them, and although she wandered restlessly from Lounge to Lounge there was no sign of them and after a while she gave up the search and retired to her own cabin.

She was quite certain that Mrs. Gladwin would disapprove, but she told herself philosophically that "what the eye does not see, the heart does not grieve over."

Nevertheless, when after midnight Yvette came to bed, she remonstrated with her.

"You might have told me where you were going," she said reproachfully.

"I did not know myself," Yvette said. "*Monsieur* Mendès whisked me away to the Writing-Room, where nobody ever goes."

"I never thought of looking there," Kelda said.

"We were hiding from you too," Yvette said mischievously.

"You know you should do nothing of the sort!" Kelda remonstrated, but in a mild tone because she was quite certain that Yvette would not listen whatever she said.

"I am enjoying myself," Yvette said, sitting down on the side of Kelda's bed and looking exquisitely lovely in a gown of coral pink with tulle of the same colour framing her white shoulders.

"You are worrying me," Kelda said.

"There is no need to worry," Yvette replied, "and quite frankly I am beginning to enjoy the voyage; even the thought of being in Dakar, at least for the next three months, is not so upsetting."

"Suppose your uncle will not let you see *Monsieur* Mendès once you have arrived?"

"I know what you are trying to say, Kelda," Yvette replied, "but I have found out everything about him and I assure you he is very respectable."

"Well, that is a relief, at any rate!"

"His father is a member of the Chamber of Deputies and Rémy has also decided to become a politician. His family is not aristocratic as the members of the old regime, like my great-aunts are, but they are well known and rich."

Yvette paused for a moment, then said:

"At least Uncle Maximus cannot say he is a fortune-hunter."

Kelda sat up in bed.

"Yvette, you are not thinking of marrying him?"

"He has not asked me yet," Yvette replied, "but

he will. He says he is in love with me and he is
also impressed by who I am. I can further his
political ambitions, if nothing else."

"And you think that is important to him?"

"Not if he is really in love with me," Yvette
said, "and he will be! Make no mistake about that,
Kelda. He will be!"

Kelda thought rather helplessly that she knew
nothing about love.

She was well aware, from the confidences Yvette
had made to her, that she had already flirted with
quite a succession of young men when she had been
on her holidays in Paris.

She had a feeling, however, that this was something more serious. Then she told herself that she
was being absurd.

Shipboard romances were notoriously fleeting,
and doubtless when they reached Dakar, Yvette
would already be bored with *Monsieur* Mendès and
be looking out for another man.

The book she had been reading before she
went to bed had told Kelda there were practically
no white women in Dakar, and she had thought
that in that case Yvette would have the choice of a
great number of men who would be only too thrilled
to see anything so attractive from the world they
had left behind.

"Rémy Mendès is gaining experience," Yvette
was saying, "which his father thinks will be of great
use to him when he too becomes a Deputy."

"So that is why he is going to Dakar?"

"Yes. As he said, as Diplomatic Equerry to the
Governor, and he has already held the same position
in Algiers."

Kelda thought eagerly that she would have liked
to talk to him about Algiers, since she had been
there, but she realised that as things were, *Monsieur*
Mendès would have no wish to talk to her when he
might be talking to Yvette.

"Of course," the latter was saying, "my aunts in Paris were talking about my making a brilliant alliance with one of the great families of France. They were even thinking of the young *Duc* de Féneon."

"If that is true," Kelda said, "then you must not involve yourself too closely with *Monsieur* Mendès."

"If I am to live with Uncle Maximus," Yvette said, as if she was working it out for herself, "I am not likely to come into contact with the *Duc* or anyone else."

"I cannot believe that your uncle wishes to tie you down in Dakar forever," Kelda objected. "Perhaps he too is thinking of your future and wishes to see you and talk to you about it."

She was well aware that French families made arranged marriages, especially when a girl was as rich and as well born as Yvette.

It was something she thought of as unpleasant, almost barbaric, but she had never said so to Yvette as she did not wish to upset her, and she knew that as far as she herself was concerned there would be no chance of marriage either arranged or otherwise.

She felt, however, that in the circumstances she ought to prevent Yvette from falling in love with a young man who had not been approved of by her relations, but how she could do that she had no idea.

The following day and the day after, she found herself sitting alone either in the Saloon or on deck, unless she sought the company of the Methodist Minister and his wife.

It was quite obvious that none of the other passengers considered her important enough even to bother to make her acquaintance.

This, Kelda knew, was due to her clothes.

She had brought with her only the grey cotton gowns that she had been made to wear at the

Seminary, and as a concession to the cold, Mrs. Gladwin had provided her with a thick black wool cape which covered her completely.

On her head she was obliged to wear the same black straw bonnet that had been modelled on those she had worn at the Orphanage.

It was exceedingly unbecoming, hiding her face and tied under her chin with cheap black ribbons.

Black gloves and sensible elastic-sided short boots completed her ensemble, and everything else she possessed went into one small bag which was so shabby that even the porters and stewards looked at it with disdain.

Kelda wasted no time being sorry for herself; indeed, she had no idea that she had anything to be sorry about.

She could hear the sea and feel the wind, and she knew with an irrepressible gladness that they were steaming towards the sunshine.

She felt as if she had been cold with the constriction in her heart from the moment her father and mother had died, until now when she was escaping from the prisons in which she had been incarcerated.

She was intelligent enough to know too that having for the first time in eight years not only enough to eat but a choice of food contributed to this new feeling of happiness.

It was also an inexpressible luxury not to have to rise at five o'clock every morning, as she had done both at the Orphanage and at the Seminary.

"I shall get fat," she told Yvette, "if I do so little and eat so much. It is something I have not been able to do for years."

"Well, I feel as if I never want to eat anything again," Yvette said, "and that is another reason why I think I must be in love."

By the time they were through the Bay of Biscay and moving down the west coast of North Africa, Yvette was no longer *thinking* she was in love.

It was obvious that she was, from the brightness of her eyes and the radiance that seemed to emanate from her whenever she and Rémy Mendès were together.

Kelda gave up begging her to be careful and not to display her affections too obviously. It was a waste of words, and when Yvette came into her bedroom at one o'clock in the morning she knew what had happened.

"I am engaged, Kelda!" she said. "Rémy and I are going to be married in Paris at Easter!"

Kelda gave a little gasp.

"But supposing Lord Orsett will not allow you to marry him?"

"Why should he stop me?" Yvette asked. "I intend to be the wife of the future Prime Minister of France, and even Uncle Maximus must be a little impressed by that."

"Suppose he is angry because you have made such an important decision without asking him first? He may not approve of *Monsieur* Mendès."

"Rémy says he will follow in the footsteps of his father, who is very important in the political world, and now that we have talked things over, I find that he is very much richer than I thought he was. We will have a house in Paris and a *Château* on his father's Estate, which is enormous! Oh, Kelda, I am so happy!"

She spoke in an ecstatic tone and Kelda's arms went out towards her.

"I am glad, dearest, I am really!" she said. "It is just that I think I am as frightened of your uncle as you are."

"I am not frightened of Uncle Maximus any more," Yvette said. "Rémy says he will look after and protect me and love me for the rest of our lives. What more can I want?"

"What indeed!" Kelda agreed.

At the same time, she was worried.

Everything she had heard about Lord Orsett

made her feel that he was not going to like decisions made without his approval, especially one that meant his niece would be staying with him for a very short time.

"We shall go to Paris at the beginning of the year," Yvette was saying, "because I intend to have a magnificent trousseau, and that, as you know, takes time."

"We?" Kelda questioned.

"You are coming with me," Yvette said. "You know I could not do without you, and you will love Paris as I do."

"What will your relations say?"

"We do not have to be concerned with my relations any more," Yvette said sweepingly, "only with Rémy, and Rémy is very grateful to you for the tactful way in which you have behaved."

The next day, after Yvette had been with Rémy all morning, she came bursting into Kelda's room just before luncheon.

"Rémy has an idea," she said, "and I think it is very sensible!"

"What is it?" Kelda asked, putting down the book she had been reading.

"It is that you should change your appearance!"

"Change my appearance?" Kelda repeated stupidly.

"I told Rémy who you were," Yvette went on, "and he is sure he has heard of your father. Anyway, he was very impressed that he had lectured to the Geographical Society, which is very highly thought of in France."

Kelda wondered what was coming next.

"Rémy is appalled," Yvette continued, "at the horrible way you have been treated by Mrs. Gladwin and the clothes you have been expected to wear. He says that we will need your support and help in facing Uncle Maximus, so you must look like someone of importance whose opinion will carry weight."

"How can I do that?" Kelda asked, not understanding what Yvette was trying to say.

"Rémy says," Yvette answered, "that people like Uncle Maximus are tremendously impressed by appearances. He has made the suggestion, and I should have thought of it before, that I should dress you in my clothes to look like the lady you are."

"B-but I could . . . not do that," Kelda said quickly, without thinking.

"Why not?" Yvette asked.

"Because they are your clothes . . . they belong to you . . . and what would Mrs. Gladwin say?"

Yvette laughed.

"Mrs. Gladwin is hundreds of miles away and personally I could not care what she says. I have heaps of dresses with me, and Rémy is right: Uncle Maximus must look upon you as an equal, otherwise he is not going to listen to anything you have to say."

"I doubt if he will listen to me anyway," Kelda said humbly.

"It is impŗ ̄tant that he should do so, at least Rémy thinks so. After all, I have been sent out to Dakar in your charge."

"Even if I look different," Kelda said after a moment, "do you not suppose that Mrs. Gladwin has told him exactly who I am and what position I occupy in her School?"

"I am sure she has done that," Yvette said with a mischievous smile, "and you will remember that as we were leaving she gave me the letter to take to Uncle Maximus. It is a pity he will never get it!"

"W-what . . . do you mean?"

"I am going to tear it up this moment and throw the pieces out of my port-hole."

"You cannot do that!" Kelda exclaimed. "It is a personal letter."

"I am sure it is full of a lot of lies," Yvette said, "but neither of us will ever know for certain because

I am not going to read it, and I will not let you read it either. It would only make you feel miserable."

She went from the cabin as she spoke, and Kelda heard her rummaging about next door.

"I have found it!" she cried after a moment.

There was the sound of tearing paper, then she came back into Kelda's cabin with a waste-paper basket in her hand.

"I am not going to open my port-hole tonight," she said, "but it is all here in minute pieces which I am going to throw into the sea first thing in the morning. Then no-one, not even the fish, will ever know what the Dragon wrote about you."

Kelda looked at her wide-eyed.

"I am sure it is ... wrong."

"On the contrary, it is right," Yvette contradicted, "and as Rémy thinks it is right, there is no argument about it. You are free, Kelda, free of that horrible old woman and everything that has happened in the past since your father and mother died."

"I ... I cannot believe it," Kelda said, and she felt the tears come into her eyes.

Yvette suddenly threw her arms round her and kissed her.

"I love you, Kelda," she said, "and if I am starting a new life, so are you. We are all going to be very happy. I am going to bed now, and tomorrow we are going to start planning my trousseau. I want to look lovely, absolutely lovely for Rémy."

The following morning as Kelda got out of bed wearing the stiff harsh calico nightgown which had been provided for her by Mrs. Gladwin, Yvette came into her cabin.

"I thought I heard you moving about," she said. "I have been too excited to sleep and so I have been sorting out a whole lot of things that you can wear until we buy some more."

"I am sure I ought not to take them," Kelda protested, but Yvette did not listen.

She brought in from her cabin a whole pile of

gowns, underclothes, and nightgowns—so many that Kelda could only gasp and find it hard to express her thanks.

"You must not give me all those!" she expostulated.

"I have enough for my immediate needs," Yvette answered, "and actually I wrote to my cousin in Paris who always helps me choose my gowns, and told her to send me as quickly as possible a whole mass of dresses which I shall need in Dakar."

"But you bought dozens in London!" Kelda exclaimed.

"London clothes are not as smart as anything that comes from Paris," Yvette replied. "But what a good thing from your point of view that I bought so much!"

That was certainly true, Kelda thought, and as she sorted out what Yvette had given her, she could hardly believe that after all these years she was actually to look what she described to herself as "a human being."

She and Yvette were the same height, but Kelda was very much thinner and she saw at once that she would have to take in the gowns at the waist.

Yvette had, as was fashionable, a small waist, very much pinched in, but Kelda's was smaller still and entirely natural.

Although Yvette insisted that Kelda should have a pair of her beautifully made French corsets, there was really no need for them, because after years of work and running up and down innumerable stairs dozens of times a day and having so little to eat, there was not a spare ounce of flesh on Kelda's body.

Only the fact that she was young and was perfectly made ensured that the curves of her breasts were very feminine, and although she was unaware of it, when she was naked she looked like a statue of a Greek goddess.

When she was finally dressed in Yvette's lace-trimmed underclothes, wearing silk stockings for the first time in her life and a gown that had cost an astronomical sum in the Rue de la Paix, she thought that she would be too shy ever to leave her cabin.

"I cannot go out like this," she said to Yvette in a kind of panic. "What will people think?"

"What people?" Yvette asked. "I doubt if those old fossils outside will even notice you! But you look very attractive, dearest Kelda, and if Rémy prefers you to me, I swear I will kill you!"

Kelda laughed.

"I think that is very unlikely," she said, "but... Yvette, I do not know how to... thank you."

Her voice broke on the words and the tears ran down her cheeks.

It was not only the clothes that were so lovely, it was that after being treated as a "Charity Child" and being crushed for so long, the transformation did something for her very spirit and she felt as if she were a phoenix rising from the ashes of herself.

Yvette hugged her.

"If you cry, you will spoil the whole effect," she said, "and I want Rémy to be stunned by your appearance. After all, it was his idea. Let us go and show him right away. He is waiting for me."

Feeling shyer than she had ever felt before, Kelda followed Yvette from their cabin to the forward Lounge where Rémy Mendès was waiting for them.

As she entered the room she saw his eyes widen for a moment in astonishment. Then he threw out his hands and cried:

"*C'est magnifique!* I congratulate you, Yvette. It is exactly how I wanted her to be!"

"You are... both so... kind," Kelda murmured, finding it difficult to speak.

"Sit down," Rémy Mendès said. "We are going to celebrate two things: first of all, *Mademoiselle* Lawrence, we are going to drink to the future of Yvette and myself. Then we are going to drink to yours, and I have a feeling it is going to be very different from what you thought it might be when you came aboard."

"If it is," Kelda said, "it is entirely thanks to you, *Monsieur*."

"I shall certainly take the credit," he said, "when your marriage follows ours."

Yvette clapped her hands together.

"You are so clever," she said. "Of course, when we go to Paris we shall find dearest Kelda a husband—someone very distinguished and very rich."

"Just like me!" Rémy said with a twinkle in his eye.

"There could not be anyone quite as wonderful as you!" Yvette said.

"I do not want you to think of me," Kelda said in a low voice, "but you know what I think about you."

They had forgotten for a moment that Kelda was there, and when she raised her glass of champagne to them she thought that she had never seen two people look so happy.

"It is like a fairy-story," she said to Yvette later that evening when she was dressing for dinner in an evening-gown that she thought was as beautiful as that which Titania herself might have worn on a midsummer's night.

"Of course it is," Yvette agreed, "and Rémy is Prince Charming and I am not only his Princess but your Fairy-Godmother!"

"I could certainly go to a Ball in this gown," Kelda said.

"But you will, of course you will. When we go to Paris there will be a Ball every night. Rémy loves dancing just as I do, and he says that when we announce our engagement his father will give the most spectacular Ball Paris has ever seen."

There were so many things to plan, and as they steamed down the coast of Africa, Yvette was busy making lists of everything she wanted to buy in Paris.

"You cannot want twenty sunshades!" Kelda expostulated.

"I hardly think twenty will be enough," Yvette replied. "After all, one with each summer ensemble, and do not forget, it will be summer almost as soon as we are married."

Only when she was alone did Kelda find herself worrying about Lord Orsett.

He did not now seem as terrifying as he had when they first boarded the ship at Southampton, when Kelda in despair had been crying every night as she remembered Mrs. Gladwin reiterating over and over again that she was to come straight home as soon as His Lordship had no further need of her services.

At the same time, when she thought about it seriously Kelda could not help feeling that Lord Orsett might easily take up the attitude that Yvette was too young to know her own mind.

She seemed, Kelda thought, older than most other girls of her age, because of the very social life she had led in Paris and also because she was intelligent.

In actual years she was not quite eighteen, and Kelda had the uncomfortable feeling that that would matter more to Lord Orsett than anything else.

She was certain that he would not be the type of person who would dig deep into somebody's character but would judge them entirely superficially.

That, she thought, was exactly what Rémy Mendès thought about him, although he was too tactful to say so. Otherwise he would not have been so insistent that she should change her appearance.

But she was deeply grateful to him for having done so.

Now she need no longer pull her hair back into a tight bun at the back of her head as Mrs. Gladwin had made her do, but could arrange it fashionably so that it looked soft and feminine, and she knew she looked more like her mother.

For the first time since she had found herself alone in the world, she felt unrestricted, as if she could behave as she wished to do.

Always before she had been forced into acting the part of a "Charity Child" who must not show that she was better bred and better taught than the other children round her, or a servant in a Seminary who must always remember to respect those who thought themselves superior to her.

Now that she could talk as an equal with Rémy Mendès and Yvette, she felt as if the years of misery had rolled away like a cloud and now she was just her father and mother's daughter.

It was as if she were travelling with them on an expedition, an adventure that was filled with laughter and gaiety because they were all together.

Every night when she said her prayers she said one of gratitude for Yvette's friendship and for what she knew was a God-given chance of escape.

"Please, God, let it go on happening," she prayed. "Do not let Lord Orsett spoil everything by sending me back to England before I have a chance to find something else to do. And ... please ... if it is possible ... let me go to Paris with Yvette ... please ... please. ..."

It was a cry that came from her very soul because it was almost impossible to have any real confidence in this new-found happiness which had come to her so unexpectedly like sunshine on a dark day.

Because she knew she would always be eternally grateful to Yvette, she prayed for her too.

"She is in love," she told God. "Let her and Rémy always love each other ... please, God ... and make Lord Orsett allow them to marry soon."

It was a prayer she said not only in her cabin at night but whenever she saw them together.

There was no doubt now that their love had grown until it was difficult for either of them to see anyone else except each other.

There was an admiration in Rémy's eyes when he looked at Yvette that could not have been anything but sincere, and Yvette loved him in a manner which told Kelda, who knew her so well, that her emotion was not just a part of her heart but of her very soul.

"They are very lucky," she told herself, "they have found what all people in the world seek—the other part of themselves—and nothing and nobody must separate them."

As she spoke, she felt almost as if she were Joan of Arc with her sword in her hand, ready to do battle for what was right and what was true.

As the idea flashed through her mind she knew that if it had to be a battle or a crusade, she was already completely and absolutely dedicated to fight it.

Chapter Three

The ship came into port at Dakar in the early afternoon.

It was very hot, but there was a soft touch of the trade winds to keep the waves dancing and to sweep away the oppression of the heat.

Kelda felt as if the golden sunshine seeped into her body, melting away the last of the cold and awakening a new vitality inside her.

Now that the moment had come when they must leave the ship, she felt as if she could not bear to say good-bye.

She wanted to go on forever, steaming away to an unknown horizon, and the fact that her whole life and outlook seemed to have changed since she came aboard made her feel as if she must say farewell to a place which had given her the security of a home.

Also, because they were nearing the moment when Yvette must meet her Guardian, she knew that they were all apprehensive and a little nervous.

Although Yvette put on a brave face and said she was no longer afraid because she was with Rémy, Kelda knew perceptively that Rémy was nervous too.

There was no doubt that he had a lot to offer the woman he would marry. At the same time, knowing how snobby the French aristocrats were, Kelda was sure that the De Villons would not think him Yvette's equal in blood.

The question was, what would Lord Orsett think?

For Kelda it was so exciting to be in Africa and have the chance of visiting a country she had never seen before that she kept wishing over and over again that her father were with her.

The coast along which they were sailing seemed flatter and lower than she had expected, but standing on deck she had been able to see shores of golden sand with coconut-trees growing down to the beach.

As they neared Dakar itself she could see that the town jutted out into the Atlantic and that there were a number of houses, more than she had expected, with trees clustered protectively round them.

The Captain of the ship had told them when they were nearing Dakar that it had a natural deep-water port.

He had spoken too of the island of Gorée, which lay within only a mile of the coast, but which he said bore the curse of the slave-trade which had made it wealthy.

Kelda had shivered as he spoke, for she had read of the horrors of slavery and the misery that those who were captured and sold suffered when they were battened down in the holds of ships and carried all over the world.

She tried not to think of their sufferings but to concentrate on looking at Dakar as the steam-ship edged its way slowly into port.

Yvette and Rémy came to join her as she stood at the rail looking at the crowds below.

"There is His Lordship's carriage waiting for you," Rémy said in a low voice.

He pointed, and Kelda and Yvette saw a very smart open carriage drawn by two horses, with a fringed white cotton awning to keep off the sun.

There was a coachman wearing an elaborate

livery which seemed somehow out-of-place in the heat, and a footman attired in the same way was standing with the crowds staring up at the ship, trying to identify those he had come to meet.

"Is my uncle with them?" Yvette asked warily.

"I cannot see him," Rémy replied, "and it would be very unlike him to meet a ship himself, whoever he was expecting as a guest."

His words brought back to Kelda the fact that Lord Orsett was said to be a recluse, and she had the uncomfortable feeling that he was already reaching out towards them, spoiling the light-hearted enjoyment with which they had spent the last week of the voyage.

She had been happy and full of laughter because she felt so different.

Every time she put on one of Yvette's beautiful gowns she felt as if it transformed not only her appearance but also her character and her personality.

Now she no longer suppressed the intelligent things she wanted to say, now she could laugh without being afraid of receiving a rebuke, and most of all she had a new confidence in herself.

Because Yvette was so kind, she no longer felt afraid all the time of what tomorrow would bring or of losing her job.

She was ashamed of herself for having been so weak and humble for so long. But she had been menaced by the fact that Mrs. Gladwin could if she wished throw her into the street without a reference and without any money to save her from starving.

It was easy to say that the knowledge that she was intelligent should have made her believe that she would find work somewhere, but who would want a "Charity Child" with nothing to recommend her except what she could say about herself?

Now everything was changed: Yvette was her friend, she was dressed as her mother would have liked to see her, and, unless all their plans were reversed, Yvette and Rémy would look after her and she would no longer be completely alone in the world.

"You are ... both so ... kind," she had said last night when once again they had toasted their future.

There had been tears in her voice and Rémy had smiled at her kindly.

"We want to be kind to you, Kelda," he said, "and I shall always be grateful to you for all you have done for my future wife."

"You know I love you," Yvette had said, "and when we reach Paris Rémy has a plan for you. He is sure one of his three sisters would love to have you teach her children English."

Kelda had with difficulty restrained her tears.

"It is like ... coming into the ... sunshine," she said, "after being enveloped in a ... fog for years and ... years."

"That is exactly what your future will be," Rémy replied. "But do not forget that tomorrow you have to meet Lord Orsett."

There was silence for a moment while all three young people were thinking what this might mean to them.

"Will you come with us to his house?" Yvette asked Rémy. "If you would, meeting him would not seem so frightening."

"I am sure that would be a mistake," Rémy replied. "He would think I was presuming. I will call formally the day after you arrive. I think it would be a mistake for you to tell him that we are engaged until after I have asked his permission to pay my addresses to you."

"I will do whatever you say," Yvette replied.

She had spoken in a low voice and Kelda could see that her eyes were troubled.

Now as the ship came nearer and nearer to the quay, Yvette hung on frantically to Rémy's arm.

"We had better go below and get ready to go ashore," Kelda said, "and do not forget that we have to thank the kind old people who have looked after us on the voyage."

"We will thank them for not doing so," Yvette said irrepressibly.

Nevertheless, she made a pretty little speech which delighted the Minister and his wife. Then, after an impassioned farewell to Rémy, she and Kelda waited in their cabin until there was a knock on the door.

When they opened it, there was an elderly man outside, very correctly dressed, who explained that he had come on behalf of Lord Orsett to escort them ashore and would collect their luggage after they had left in the carriage for His Lordship's mansion.

They started down the gangway, Yvette looking over her shoulder as she went for one last glimpse of Rémy. Then the crowds moved aside for them to walk to the carriage.

After the elderly man had helped them into it, the footman jumped up on the box and the horses started off.

Now as they drove down the tree-bordered streets Kelda had a chance to look at the people, and she realised that they were very different from those she had seen when she was in Algiers.

The first thing she noticed was the kaleidoscope of colour shown in the voluminous *boubous* of the native women.

In brilliant blues, purples, greens, and pinks, they swept along the roadside looking like huge flowers, their heads swathed in colourful turbans, their feet bare, their wrists weighed down with jingling bangles.

If the women were impressive, Kelda thought, the men were undoubtedly magnificent.

Very tall, they had the broadest shoulders she had ever seen, tapering down to narrow hips, and they walked with an athletic grace which again made them different from any other natives she had seen in other parts of the world.

'Papa would be able to tell me about them and their different tribes,' she thought.

She wondered if Lord Orsett, when she met him, would answer the questions she longed to ask.

They drove almost in silence for quite some way until the houses were left behind, and now they were moving along what seemed nothing but a dusty track, with the sea on their left.

The land rose until there were cliffs down to the water's edge.

It was then, suddenly, that Kelda saw in front of them what she thought at first must be a mosque or some civic building.

It was surrounded by trees except for the side that looked out towards the sea, and when the road ended with large wrought-iron gates tipped with gold, she knew they had reached what Yvette had called her uncle's "Palace."

It certainly looked like one, dazzlingly white in the sunshine.

It was almost like a Georgian house in England, except that its long windows and its ornamentation gave it an undoubtedly Eastern look.

There was a flag flying over the pillared portico which Kelda suspected was Lord Orsett's personal standard, and as they swept up to the entrance she saw that the hibiscus-shrubs with their brilliant crimson blossoms made it appear almost as if the white building were being consumed by flames.

"It is certainly very lovely!" she exclaimed.

"I am . . . frightened," Yvette murmured.

"I am sure there is no need to be," Kelda replied, although she was far from feeling as confident as she sounded. "Your uncle certainly appreciates beauty if nothing else."

She knew that Yvette wanted to say that that was not particularly comforting, but at that moment the carriage drew up beside a flight of steps covered with a red carpet.

Servants, wearing white on the front of which

was embellished Lord Orsett's coat-of-arms in red, appeared in the doorway.

Yvette got out slowly and Kelda followed her.

She could not help feeling thankful that she was not wearing the ugly clothes in which Mrs. Gladwin had expected her to appear.

Instead she had chosen for her arrival a pale green gown of Yvette's which made her look very young and spring-like.

The hat she wore was decorated with white roses and green leaves that were the colour of the gown, and she thought she made the perfect foil for Yvette, who was in pink, in which Rémy liked her better than in any other colour.

It was a very elaborate gown, almost too elaborate, Kelda thought, but she knew Yvette wanted to appear at her best, and not only was her hat decorated with roses but they also appeared on the small sunshade she carried, which had a handle of pink quartz.

"You look lovely, dearest!" Kelda had told Yvette, and she thought Lord Orsett must be made of stone if he did not appreciate how pretty and attractive his niece was.

A servant who was obviously in command of the rest invited them, in French, to follow him and took them through a large Hall.

As in most large houses in tropical parts of the world there were doors at each end of it, which were left wide open so that what wind there was could blow to cool the building even at the hottest part of the day.

Through the other door Kelda could see the blue of the sea and she knew that Lord Orsett's house, high on the cliffs, would have a view she would enjoy.

But for the moment she was too apprehensive of what he himself would be like to be interested in anything else.

A servant opened the door to the left of them,

and as he did so, Kelda saw what seemed to be an enormous room with six long windows opening out onto a terrace.

The sun-blinds were halfway down to keep out the sun, and the room itself was dim and cool so that for the moment it was hard to see if it was occupied, until at the far end she saw a man rise to his feet and knew it was Lord Orsett.

Yvette walked ahead of her, then as Kelda followed she saw Lord Orsett for the first time and found him very different from what she had imagined.

To begin with, from the way Yvette always spoke of him she had thought he must be a man of fifty or more, but instead he was much younger and had a physique which could rival that of any of the natives she had admired as they drove from the port.

Broad-shouldered and dressed in a white suit, he seemed large and overpowering. Then as she looked at his face she was startled.

His features were clear-cut and he looked handsome in an aristocratic and typically English manner. At the same time he also appeared cynical and stern to the point of grimness.

He was looking at Yvette and Kelda thought with a little shiver that he appeared to be inspecting her almost dispassionately without a vestige of affection.

It was a critical appraisal, she thought, and there was something unnatural and almost unpleasant about it.

"Welcome to Dakar, Yvette," Lord Orsett said in a deep voice which somehow contrived to be cold and impersonal. "I hope you had a pleasant voyage."

Yvette curtseyed.

"Very pleasant, thank you, Uncle Maximus. May I present my friend, Kelda Lawrence, who accompanied me on the voyage?"

Lord Orsett turned his attention to Kelda, who

also curtseyed and who found it hard to meet his eyes, although she forced herself to do so.

"Friend?" he queried. "I instructed the woman who runs your School to send a mistress with you."

"They all refused to come so far as—Africa."

There was a little pause before Yvette said the last word, and Kelda knew she was about to say "such an outlandish place" but checked herself at the last moment.

"But Miss Lawrence was more obliging," Lord Orsett remarked.

He did not make it sound very complimentary, and Kelda said:

"It has been a privilege, My Lord."

"Kelda is used to travelling, Uncle Maximus," Yvette said quickly, as if she was conscious of his disapproval. "Her father was Philip Lawrence, the Archaeologist, and she visited many places with him before he died."

"Indeed!"

Lord Orsett did not sound interested and both girls were conscious of his disapproval that Yvette was not accompanied by a woman older than Kelda.

"I must offer you some refreshment," he said. "It is hot at this time of the day and most people make it an excuse for a *siesta*."

He spoke as if this was a weakness to which he would not succumb, but before Yvette or Kelda could say anything the door opened and servants came in carrying a tray on which were long, cool drinks and small sweetmeats to eat, which Kelda found delicious.

They sat down on the sofas and chairs which were so large and comfortable that Kelda was certain Lord Orsett must have chosen them himself.

She took a quick glance round the room and decided that if he loved beauty outside his house, he certainly enjoyed both beauty and comfort in it.

The room was furnished in exquisite taste with paintings on the walls which she was sure were exceptional, and what was unusual was that the room was uncluttered, unlike what she knew was fashionable in most houses in England.

There were some fine pieces of china, and carvings which she was certain had been done by native craftsmen, but otherwise the room with its fine proportions had a cool emptiness which she knew, as her father had told her, was characteristic of the great Architects who had built in the Eighteenth Century.

However, it was difficult to think of anything except their host.

He sat back at his ease, but it would have been impossible to ignore him, Kelda thought, because his very personality seemed to exude strength and power, and something else which made her afraid.

She tried to analyse what it was and thought it might be a kind of domination of will, as if he was so determined to have his own way that one felt drawn to him irresistibly, as if by a magnet.

"What do you think of him?" Yvette asked a little later, when they had been shown to their bedrooms.

"I think he is exceedingly frightening," Kelda replied, before she had time to consider her words.

"So now you know how I am feeling," Yvette said. "How can I tell him, how can I possibly tell him, Kelda, that I am engaged to Rémy?"

"I should say nothing," Kelda advised, "until Rémy calls on you tomorrow."

"I am sure that is wise," Yvette said with a little sigh. "I feel if we argue with him he would crush us as if we were insects beneath his foot."

That, Kelda thought, was true, but she knew it would be wise not to say so.

She suddenly felt that both she and Yvette were somehow small and very insignificant.

Here they were in Africa, and unless Lord Orsett agreed to what they wished, they were, to all intents and purposes, prisoners in this magnificent mansion, and there was no-one to whom they could appeal for help or even for advice.

Then she decided she was frightening herself unnecessarily, and on no account must Yvette know what she was thinking.

Instead she went to the window to look out at what she had known would be an exquisitely beautiful view.

The Atlantic, glorious and blue as the Madonna's robe, lay in front of her, ending in a misty horizon where the sea met the sky.

To the left she could just see the island of Gorée and to the right the coastline stretched away, golden with sand and green with coconut-trees.

The fishermen were putting out to sea in pointed little boats which she had read were called "pirogues."

There was something delicate and romantic about them and she wondered if she would ever have the chance to go in one.

Behind her, sitting on the bed which looked as large and luxurious as the rest of the room, Yvette was talking.

Kelda turned from the window.

"You did not tell me," she said, "that your uncle was so young. I expected a much older man, at least old enough to be your father."

"He seems very old to me."

"How old is he?"

"I think about thirty-six or thirty-seven," Yvette replied, "and that is old enough in all conscience."

Kelda smiled.

"He would not be flattered to hear you say so."

"I do not suppose he would care what I thought or said about him," Yvette replied petulantly. "You can see what he is like: completely engrossed in himself and his own consequence. Rémy says he is not liked by any of the young men in Dakar because he condescends to them, but he is a friend of the Governor-General."

"I expect he condescends to him too," Kelda

replied. "I wonder why he should stay here when he is English. After all, it is a French Colony."

"I suppose as my aunt was French he prefers the French to the English. Some people do, you know."

Yvette was teasing Kelda because she had often laughed at her for being patriotic and proud of her own country.

"What have the English ever done for you," she had asked once, "except shove you into an Orphanage?"

"Whatever they do or do not do, I am still English," Kelda had replied.

"And I am French, thank Heaven!" Yvette had said proudly.

"We should walk about with our flags sewn on us," Kelda had said.

And both had laughed.

Now, thinking of Lord Orsett, she felt that as an Englishman he should be living in his own country.

'Surely he has houses and Estates in England if he is as rich as they say he is,' she thought. 'Why should he want to spend his money in Dakar?'

It was a mystery and she thought she was never likely to get an answer to her question.

"Do you suppose we ought to go downstairs and talk to Uncle Maximus?" Yvette asked.

"It would be polite," Kelda answered. "I would like to see the rest of the house, and if it is cool enough perhaps we could sit out on the terrace and look at the sea."

"I hate the sea!" Yvette replied. "I want to look out a window and see the roofs of Paris. I want Rémy to take me dancing. I want to hear the conversation and the gossip of people who enjoy life, which, as you can see for yourself, is something Uncle Maximus does not do."

"Then why does he stay here?" Kelda asked.

"Only he can answer that question, but I doubt if you would get a truthful answer out of him."

"Let us go down and try," Kelda suggested.

They went down the stairs and when they reached the Hall the head-servant told them that he had been instructed by His Lordship to show them any part of the house they wished to see. Then there would be tea waiting for them on the terrace.

It was a relief that they would be able to look at everything without being accompanied by their host, and as they went from one huge, beautiful room to another Kelda knew that she had been right in thinking Lord Orsett had exceptionally good taste.

He had managed to combine things he had brought from Europe with those that he had either collected or had made for him in Senegal.

There were carvings about which she would like to be able to talk to someone knowledgeable, knowing they were very old and doubtless steeped in the legends of Africa.

There were metals that she thought must be precious and weavings which had a special charm of their own.

There were many things she wanted to stop and examine, but she saw that Yvette was bored and she told herself there would be plenty of time later.

They hurried on and finally found themselves on the terrace with what was almost an English tea waiting for them served by several servants.

"Do you think Uncle Maximus ever entertains people here?" Yvette asked. "There is plenty of room to do so."

"It was you who told me he was a recluse," Kelda replied.

"That is what they said in Paris, and Rémy told me that with the exception that he sometimes dines with the Governor-General, he never appears to go anywhere."

"What does he do all the time?"

Yvette shrugged her shoulders.

"Perhaps he just sits hating everybody, or practising some special magic of his own."

Kelda did not reply and after a moment Yvette said:

"You have not forgotten that I want to use Black Magic on him? But I have a feeling that it would have to be very strong and very potent."

"Let us hope you will get everything you want without resorting to any such tactics," Kelda replied.

At the same time, she thought that Lord Orsett was a very mysterious man.

Because the house was so big, she had the feeling that she and Yvette were isolated in it, even while she told herself that it was ridiculous to think such a thing.

There was no sign of Lord Orsett after they had finished tea, when the head-servant appeared again to tell them that their luggage had arrived and was being unpacked and that dinner would be at eight o'clock.

Yvette merely nodded to show that she understood what she had been told, but Kelda asked:

"Where shall we meet His Lordship before dinner?"

"I will be waiting, *M'mselle*, at the foot of the stairs to escort you to whichever room His Lordship wishes to receive you in."

"Thank you," Kelda said.

She rose to her feet as she spoke, then she and Yvette went upstairs.

Because it was so early in the year, darkness came swiftly and by five o'clock it was already much cooler than it had been all day.

They had celebrated Christmas Day at sea, and while the staff on the steam-ship had done their best to make it a festive occasion and there had been crackers to pull and small souvenirs brought in by "Father Christmas" for all the guests, the passengers had been mostly too old or too dull to make it really amusing.

Kelda, however, had enjoyed it although Yvette and Rémy had been too interested in each other to want to take part.

They had not listened to the Concert that had taken place in the Lounge, although they had danced to the Band that had played later in the evening.

Now in the sunshine of Dakar it was difficult to think that in England there were still frost, snow, ice, and hail-storms, and that if she were still at the Seminary she would be shivering at night in the garret in which she slept because Mrs. Gladwin would never provide her with enough blankets.

Upstairs they found two maids in each room unpacking their gowns.

They were pretty black girls dressed in cotton gowns such as housemaids wore in England, but with their heads swathed in red turbans, obviously to match the large red insignia worn by the men-servants.

"His Lordship undoubtedly likes colour," Kelda said when she and Yvette were alone and the maids had withdrawn.

"Why should you say that?" Yvette asked.

"His servants are so colourful, and there is lots of colour in the rooms, although they give the impression of being all white."

"What are you suggesting we should do about it?" Yvette asked. "Paint our faces the colours of the rainbow?"

"No, not that," Kelda said with a smile, "but wear one of your brighter gowns this evening. You know we have to make a good impression on him."

"I will wear the cherry-coloured tulle which Rémy likes."

"In which case I will wear the blue chiffon you gave me."

"Do you think that is smart enough for His Lordship?" Yvette teased.

"You are the important person!" Kelda answered. "And personally I admire myself so much in the lovely clothes you have given me that it does not worry me what His Lordship thinks one way or the other."

"I wish I could say the same."

Yvette gave a little groan and added:

"Just think, Kelda, if I had not met Rémy how miserable I should be feeling at this moment. Supposing I thought I had to be shut up here for years and years with no-one to talk to except Uncle Maximus?"

"There must be Europeans living in Dakar."

"Only men, and according to Rémy, Uncle Maximus never asks anyone to his house who is young. Rémy has only been here twice, when he accompanied the Governor-General for some reason or another."

Kelda did not reply, but she could understand what Yvette was saying and she thought that anyone so full of life and energy would doubtless find it extremely dull after she had known the gaieties of Paris.

When she was dressed for dinner and stood for a moment at the window looking at the moonlight touching the waves and turning them to silver, and the sky filled with stars that twinkled like diamonds in the darkness, she wished that she at any rate could stay in Dakar for a long time.

To her the alternative was not Paris and parties, it was humiliation and hard work in the Seminary.

As she thought of it she said a little prayer of gratitude because, whatever happened in the future, for the moment everything was different from what it had been for eight long, miserable years.

They went down the stairs and the servant who was waiting took them down a wide cool corridor to a room they had not previously visited when they had toured the house.

It had long windows which overlooked both the sea and the land, although it was too dark to see anything outside.

As it happened, Kelda had eyes only for the room itself. Unlike the rest of the house, large though it was, it was filled with books on every wall and books were also stacked on tables and even on the floor.

"I thought perhaps you would like to see my special Sanctum where I spend most of my time," Lord Orsett said to Yvette, "so I have invited you here this evening, although I doubt if you will have many invitations to join me here in the future."

"Why is that?" Yvette enquired.

"Because this is where I work."

"What sort of work?"

"I am writing a history of the West African tribes."

Kelda made an involuntary little sound of excitement and Lord Orsett turned towards her.

"That surprises you, Miss Lawrence?"

"I am extremely interested, My Lord. When I saw the carvings you have, I longed to know all about them, and I felt certain that they had a long history, just as I am sure the legends of West Africa are fascinating."

Lord Orsett looked surprised, then he said almost sharply to Yvette:

"And are you as interested, Yvette, as your friend is?"

"I am more interested in the present than the past," Yvette replied. "If I have to, I would rather study the history of Paris than anywhere else."

She spoke provocatively and Lord Orsett frowned.

Kelda knew that Yvette had annoyed him, and he said abruptly:

"I thought perhaps you would like a glass of wine before dinner, and as you have such a penchant for Paris, it is perhaps appropriate that I can offer you a glass of champagne."

"Thank you," Yvette said. "When were you last in Paris, Uncle Maximus?"

"A long time ago," Lord Orsett replied, "and it is a city to which I have no intention of ever returning."

There was no disguising the contemptuous way he spoke.

"How can you say something like that?" Yvette exclaimed. "Paris is the most wonderful, most exciting city in the world!"

"I presume you have seen a great many others with which to compare it," Lord Orsett said, sneering.

"Enough to know what I like, and where I want to live," Yvette answered.

Her uncle did not reply, and watching him Kelda thought his eyes were suddenly steel-like and his lips had tightened into a hard line.

'Yvette is antagonising him,' she thought, and because she was determined to be conciliatory, she said:

"Are all your books in here about Africa?"

"Most of them," Lord Orsett replied.

"Then I hope you will allow me to read some of them which will tell me what I want to know; otherwise I might bore you by asking too many questions."

"Most of the books are written in French," he replied in an uncompromising voice.

"I can read French quite competently," Kelda said.

She thought by his expression that he did not believe her, but he replied politely:

"In which case I can certainly find you some literature on subjects about which you are particularly curious."

It was a relief when dinner was announced and they went into a large room in which it would have been easy to entertain fifty or even a hundred people without being overcrowded.

The meal was original and delicious, and because Kelda was afraid that Yvette might antagonise her uncle even further than she had already, she put herself out to ask about the food.

He told her the names of the local fish and she learnt that small cherry-tomatoes were one of the favourite products of the district.

It was a conversation that interested her, but she knew, by Yvette's expression and the manner in which she made no effort to join in, that she was bored.

In fact, when after dinner was over they moved into a Reception-Room where they had been before, she yawned several times and Kelda wondered if it would be wise to suggest that they retire to bed.

With a glass of brandy in his hand, Lord Orsett sat down beside her, and when there was silence for a moment Kelda felt instinctively that he was going to say something of importance.

"You must have wondered, Yvette," he said after a moment, "why I ordered you to come out here to me when I was well aware that you were expecting to go to Paris to live with your French uncles and aunts."

"I thought it very strange, Uncle Maximus," Yvette replied, "and quite frankly, I was upset."

"That is what I expected," Lord Orsett said, "but now I am going to explain to you why I wanted you in Dakar."

He looked at her as he spoke, and it was, Kelda felt, as if once again he was appraising her as a man might look at a horse, noting her points, her appearance, from her shining dark hair to her small, exquisitely shod feet.

"The truth is, Yvette," he said after a moment, "that I have brought you here to be married."

"Married?"

The word was barely audible as Yvette spoke, and yet to Kelda it sounded like a cry that echoed and re-echoed round the room.

"Yes, married," Lord Orsett repeated, "and let me explain why."

He sat back a little more comfortably in his chair and Kelda thought he was well aware that both her eyes and Yvette's were fixed on him with an almost terrified attention.

"I have been living here," Lord Orsett said, "for some years, and I have become extremely interested in the special problem of French colonisation in Senegal, which is different from any other part of the French Empire."

He paused as if he expected one or the other of them to speak, and when they did not do so, he continued:

"Senegal is now France's major base in West Africa, and it is here that her Imperialism will prove most successful."

"What has that to do with—me?" Yvette managed to ask.

"That is what I will tell you in due course," Lord Orsett replied. "I have discussed the French ambitions for Senegal with the present Governor-General, who is a very intelligent man, and with a number of officials who have come here from France in the last two years. What they think is wanted more than anything else at the moment is a stable white society both in Dakar and in St. Louis."

He looked at Kelda as he asked:

"You seem to have an interest in West Africa, so I presume you are aware of the difficulties that have occurred amongst those administering the country, owing to the absence of European women?"

"I can ... understand that being a ... problem," Kelda answered. "At the same time, I am not aware of any of the ... details."

"Then let me inform you of the position to date," Lord Orsett said. "Inevitably, the French who settled here, either for a long or a short term, took African mistresses and wives."

Yvette gave a little gasp as if she was shocked, but she did not speak and Lord Orsett went on:

"The wives, *signares* as they were called, of European husbands in trading-posts have a certain social status as consorts."

"I think I read that ... somewhere," Kelda said, feeling that she was expected to say something.

"A soldier or company employee sometimes sets his *signare* up in business to augment his own salary, and if he leaves the post indefinitely, his business and property are left to her and her children."

"That seems fair," Kelda murmured.

She was talking because she felt that if she held Lord Orsett's attention he would not notice that Yvette had gone very pale and was clenching her fingers together until the knuckles were white.

"The French have decided that this position is not particularly satisfactory," Lord Orsett went on. "As they wish to develop Dakar as an important port, it is obvious that European women must be persuaded to live here, and their presence will have a marked effect on the character of society."

"I can ... understand that," Kelda said in a low voice.

"At the moment there are considerably fewer than a hundred white women in the whole of Dakar. This is why the French intend to make every possible effort to put pressure on traders and employees of the Government to bring their wives here, so that they can persuade other women to join their husbands overseas."

He paused, but as Kelda did not speak, he went on:

"There will be plenty for them to do and the

Governor-General himself is determined to set an example which he is sure will be followed by a number of other officials."

There was silence until Kelda asked in a voice little above a whisper:

"How . . . how does he . . . intend to do . . . that?"

"The Governor-General was widowed some years ago and intends to marry again," Lord Orsett said.

He turned his head to look at Yvette.

"I have given him my permission to pay his addresses to you, Yvette, and he will call on you tomorrow."

Yvette was obviously paralysed into immobility, but Kelda spoke for her.

"The Governor-General? But surely he is an . . . old man?"

"He is certainly somewhere between fifty and sixty years of age," Lord Orsett answered, "but he is young at heart, healthy, and athletic, and my niece will have a position not only of importance but one in which she can set an example which I know will have a resounding effect throughout the whole of France."

"Are you really—expecting me to—marry an old man and—live in this—ghastly, uncivilised place?" Yvette asked.

She was so shocked that the words seemed almost to sputter from her lips and were barely coherent.

"You will take a different view of Dakar when you have lived here for some time," Lord Orsett replied, "and I assure you that many women would welcome the opportunity of marrying such a distinguished man."

"Then let—them have him!" Yvette cried, and now her voice was hysterical. "I have no—intention of marrying the—Governor-General or of—staying in Dakar, and—you cannot—make me do so!"

She had risen as she spoke, and now she faced

her uncle defiantly, her whole body quivering with the intensity of her feelings.

"I think you are mistaken about that," Lord Orsett said in a quiet voice. "I can and will make you do what I wish you to do. I am your Guardian and you are completely dependent upon me until you come of age."

"If you think because of that you can—force me into a—marriage to a man I have never seen—a man who is—old enough to be my father, you are very much mistaken."

Yvette drew a deep breath and added:

"As it happens, I was going to tell you—tomorrow—that I am—engaged to *Monsieur* Rémy Mendès, and I will marry no-one—no-one—else but him!"

Yvette's voice rang out, and as if the mere mention of Rémy's name gave her courage, she faced Lord Orsett defiantly and the colour came back into her cheeks.

"And who is this Rémy Mendès?" Lord Orsett enquired.

"As it happens, he is Diplomatic Equerry to your—precious Governor-General, and when you meet him you will understand that he is a very suitable husband for me, and not a—man with one foot in the—grave."

"It is for me to decide whether or not he is suitable," Lord Orsett said in a lofty tone. "Where did you meet him?"

"Coming here on the ship."

"A shipboard romance? That is easily forgotten."

Lord Orsett spoke sneeringly and Kelda thought it was what she might have expected.

"That is—where you are—mistaken," Yvette said. "I love Rémy with all my heart and he loves me."

"You are convinced that your quite considerable fortune has nothing to do with it?"

"That is the sort of thing you would think," Yvette

said rudely. "Rémy's father is an extremely rich man. He is also a member of the Chamber of Deputies. He will show you his credentials tomorrow. Then you can see for yourself what he is like."

"He need not waste his time," Lord Orsett said.

"What do you mean by that?" Yvette asked.

"I mean, to put it bluntly, that I have no intention of having my plans disrupted in any way. You will marry the Governor-General and we will have no more nonsense about impecunious suitors who, if your companion had been doing her job properly, would not have been allowed to approach you in the first place."

"You really think you can force this ridiculous idea upon me?" Yvette asked furiously.

"I am quite sure I can," Lord Orsett replied. "I have brought you here to be married, and married you will be within the next three weeks. And make no mistake, if this unimportant Frenchman tries to communicate with you tomorrow or at any other time while you are a guest in my house, I will deal with him in a manner which he will bitterly regret for the rest of his life."

Yvette lost her temper.

"How dare you! How dare you threaten me—a citizen of France! You have no right in this country in the first place, and you are both mad and bad, as everybody has said you are! If you think you can order me round as if I were a native servant, you are very much mistaken!"

She stamped her foot as she said:

"I hate you, Uncle Maximus! I have always hated you! I would drown myself rather than let you do anything that you have suggested!"

As she spoke, almost screaming the last words at him, Yvette turned and ran from the room.

She left the door open and Kelda could hear her running down the corridor.

She rose, and as she would have followed

Yvette, Lord Orsett, who was still lying back comfortably in his chair, asked:

"Have you nothing to say, Miss Lawrence?"

Kelda knew he spoke provocatively.

She turned around to look at him, her eyes very large in her small face.

"If you want the truth, My Lord," she said, "I think what you have suggested is diabolical! It is flying in the face of nature for any man, however important socially, to play at being God."

Lord Orsett did not reply. He only glared at her and Kelda glared back.

Then, without another word, she turned and went from the room, also leaving the door open behind her.

Chapter Four

As Kelda went slowly up the stairs, holding on to the bannisters, she realised she was trembling and her heart was thumping in her breast.

She felt as if she, as well as Yvette, had passed through a traumatic experience which had left her both shaken and shocked.

It seemed inconceivable that Lord Orsett could have thought out anything so horrible, indeed as she had said diabolical, for someone as charming and sweet as Yvette.

The fact that he had obviously not given any thought to his niece as a person, but merely as a puppet to implement his plans, made it worse.

Everything Yvette had said about him seemed to Kelda to be an understatement of what he was really like.

By the time she had reached the top of the stairs and turned along the corridor towards her bedroom, Kelda was thinking frantically not only of what she would say to Yvette but of what they could do.

As she expected, Yvette was lying face downwards on her bed, sobbing her heart out.

She sat down on the bed beside her and Yvette turned to fling her arms around Kelda saying as she did so:

"Save me—Kelda, oh—save me! You know I—have to marry—Rémy."

"Yes, I know that," Kelda said, "and that is why you must stop crying and we must try to see what we can do to circumvent your uncle's wickedness."

She spoke so positively that Yvette's tears stopped and she looked at Kelda questioningly.

"You really—mean you will—help me?" she asked, with a sob in her voice that was infinitely pathetic.

"Of course I will help you," Kelda said determinedly, "but we have to be clever about this. We must remember where we are and how powerful your uncle is."

Yvette took her arms from round Kelda's neck and sat back against the pillows.

"I have never seen you like this before."

"Like what?" Kelda asked absent-mindedly.

"So strong and brave. I always thought you were weak because you let yourself be bullied by Mrs. Gladwin."

"But now I am fighting not for myself but for you," Kelda answered, "and that is a very different thing."

"And you think you—will be able to—help me?"

There was behind the question a desperation of which Kelda was well aware.

"You know, without my saying so, that it is not going to be easy," she replied, "but there is Rémy, and the first thing we must do is get in touch with him."

"But how? How?" Yvette asked. "You know Uncle Maximus is going to insult him, and you can be quite —certain that he will not allow him to—write to me, let alone—see me."

"I have thought of that already," Kelda said. "I cannot believe that Rémy will submit tamely to losing you, and you will have to be not only courageous about this but also clever and subtle."

"How can I?" Yvette asked. "Tell me what to do."

Kelda was silent for a moment, staring at the carving on the bed-head but not seeing it.

Instead she saw the radiance on Rémy's face and on Yvette's which had been there when they looked at each other on board ship, and she had known that this was love as she had always thought it must be, if it was real and came from both the heart and the soul.

'I must save them both,' she thought.

She felt a violent, fiery anger rise within her at the thought of what Lord Orsett was trying to do.

"Tell me what you are—thinking," Yvette said in a frightened voice.

"I was thinking," Kelda replied after a moment, "that if you are to marry Rémy, he will have to take you away from here, and quickly!"

"Do you think he can do that?"

"He will have to, otherwise your uncle will force you into marriage with the Governor-General."

Yvette gave a little cry of sheer horror.

"To marry anyone other than Rémy would make me want to kill myself," she said. "Even to speak of marriage with an old man makes my flesh—creep, and I feel as if I—might be—sick."

"I can understand that," Kelda said gently. "At the same time, we have to realise that you are under the jurisdiction of your Guardian and Rémy is under the Governor-General."

"It is only a temporary appointment," Yvette said quickly.

"I know that," Kelda answered, "but we are in Dakar, and the Governor-General, who is all-powerful, could have him put in prison or sent back summarily to France and there would be nothing we could do about it."

She saw the stricken look in Yvette's eyes and said quickly:

"That is why the first thing we have to do is, I am sure, to deceive your uncle into believing that you will do what he wants."

"Do what he—wants?"

Yvette's voice rose almost to a scream.

"You must pretend to agree to his plans," Kelda said. "If he thinks you are fighting him and opposing him, he will watch everything you do and there will be no chance whatsoever of escaping his surveillance."

Yvette realised that what she was saying was sensible, and her eyes were fixed on Kelda as she said almost beneath her breath:

"Go on!"

"We must make plans quickly," Kelda said, "and I think the first thing must be for you to apologise to your uncle for your outburst and say that you were taken by surprise, but that you are prepared to consider what he suggests. The next step will be to receive the Governor-General when he calls tomorrow."

"Do you think Uncle Maximus will be deceived into thinking that I will—obey him?"

"It depends on how well you act the part," Kelda said. "What we must not do is to make the Governor-General antagonistic towards Rémy."

"No—no—of course not."

"I may be wrong," Kelda went on, "but I have the feeling that when he reaches the Palace he will learn, if not from the Governor-General himself then from the other Equerries and Aides-de-Camp, what is being planned for you. I cannot believe that they are not aware of what the Governor-General and your uncle have in mind for the Colony."

"What will Rémy think when he knows it is—intended that I shall—marry someone else?"

The question was pathetic and Kelda said firmly:

"I believe he will be as shocked as you are, and he also will be determined to do something about it."

"He loves me! I know he loves me!" Yvette cried.

"I too am sure of that," Kelda said, "and somehow he will get in touch with us, however difficult it may be."

"Uncle Maximus will prevent it."

"Rémy will be aware that he will try to do so," Kelda said.

Yvette wiped away the last remaining tears from her eyes.

"Tell me what I am to do," she pleaded. "Tell me exactly, so that I shall not make any mistakes."

* * *

It was a pale and subdued Yvette who walked demurely downstairs beside Kelda the following morning.

They had learnt from the servants that breakfast would be served on the terrace, and as they stepped out to where the meal was laid under a red striped awning, Lord Orsett rose at their approach.

He was wearing riding-breeches, with a well-tied stock round his neck, but the white linen coat he had obviously been wearing was thrown over an adjacent chair.

He looked strong, masculine, and, as Kelda had expected, very overpowering.

His eyes were on Yvette as she advanced towards him, and when she reached him he said:

"Good-morning, Yvette! I trust you slept well."

"Quite well, thank you, Uncle Maximus, and I would like to—apologise for being so—rude last night. You took me by—surprise and I was—frightened. I hope you will—forgive me."

Her words and her conciliatory tone, Kelda could see, took Lord Orsett by surprise.

For a moment he raised his eye-brows. Then he said:

"Perhaps I was somewhat precipitate on your

first evening, and as you have made me an apology, I hope you will accept mine."

"Of course, Uncle Maximus," Yvette said, "and it is far too lovely a day to—quarrel with anyone."

"That is what we both should think," Lord Orsett said, "and tomorrow I shall be delighted if you and Miss Lawrence will come riding with me. It is always most pleasant early in the morning before it grows hot."

"That would be delightful!" Kelda interposed. "I so want to see the wild land outside the town, which I am told is very beautiful."

"It is indeed," Lord Orsett said.

As they seated themselves at the table, he said as if he suddenly remembered that he should enquire after Kelda's well-being:

"I hope you too, Miss Lawrence, spent a good night."

"I slept well, My Lord, because, like Yvette, I was tired after being at sea for so long; and may I say I find the waves more attractive when they are murmuring in the distance than when they are rolling beneath me."

Lord Orsett smiled.

"Are you telling me that you were sea-sick?"

"Surprisingly, neither of us suffered from that unfortunate complaint," Kelda replied, "but it was very uncomfortable in the Bay of Biscay."

"That is what I always find," he replied.

The servants brought breakfast and Yvette made a brave attempt to eat.

When they were alone again Lord Orsett said:

"I have received a message from the Palace to say that the Governor-General will call on us at noon. I hope you will assist me to greet him."

"Of course, Uncle Maximus."

Yvette spoke quite naturally, then she said:

"Uncle Maximus, it will make me feel shy if the moment we—meet and before we are even—acquainted, you speak of more—intimate matters."

As if he was relieved that she was being so pliable, Lord Orsett said quickly:

"Naturally, I understand, and this will just be a friendly call so that you and His Excellency can meet each other. He is an interesting and extremely intelligent man and I feel sure you will have many tastes in common."

"Does he come from Paris?" Yvette asked.

"He was not born there, but I believe he lived there for some years of his life," Lord Orsett informed her. "He has also held important posts in other French Provinces besides Senegal."

"I shall look forward to hearing about them," Yvette said.

She was acting so well that Kelda had to resist an impulse to clap for what was in fact an extremely convincing performance.

It had taken a long time, in fact half the night, for her and Yvette to work out exactly what she should do and what she should say.

It was not only because Yvette was intelligent, but because she loved Rémy so passionately, that she was prepared to make every possible effort to do what Kelda suggested.

Kelda was aware now, as they went on talking, that Lord Orsett was agreeably surprised at the way Yvette was behaving and was undoubtedly beginning to believe that the scene last night was just the result of a shock that he should not have caused in the first place.

As Kelda had said to Yvette last night:

"We know one thing which will be helpful, and that is that your uncle has had very little to do with women since your aunt died."

"What about the one my cousin saw when she was here?"

"I do not think that she could have been of any great importance," Kelda said quickly.

"Do you think that she was one of the women he talked about last night?"

"I have no idea," Kelda replied, "but anyway it is obvious that she is not here now. I cannot believe that, if you are prepared to be contrite and ready to please him, he will not be completely deceived."

This, she was sure, was what was now happening, and while she recognised that there were little discrepancies in what Yvette said which might have made a man more knowledgeable in the ways of women suspicious, she was certain that Lord Orsett was completely deceived.

"What would you like to do now?" he asked when breakfast was over.

Yvette looked at Kelda, who already had another idea which she thought was important.

"If it would not be any trouble," she said, "Yvette and I would love to drive round the town. Actually there are one or two things we would like to buy sometime, not particularly today but when it is convenient."

She thought for a moment that Lord Orsett gave her a sharp look, then he said:

"Perhaps you would like to drive with me in my new curricle, which has recently been delivered from France. It is, I am told, what dashing young Frenchmen who fancy themselves with the reins use when they drive in the Bois."

Kelda saw Yvette stiffen as he spoke of Paris, and because she was afraid she might betray her longing for the city that meant so much to her, Kelda said quickly.

"That would be lovely! There is so much I want to see in this beautiful country."

She thought for a moment that Lord Orsett looked at her with approval.

Then, as if Yvette felt it was expected of her, she said:

"I would enjoy it too, Uncle Maximus, and I am sure that you have fine horses. I think I remember Mama saying how fond you were of riding."

"You are quite right, Yvette," Lord Orsett said. "I have managed to find myself some excellent horse-flesh, as you will see when you both ride with me tomorrow. You have riding-habits with you, of course?"

"Of course," Kelda replied, hoping as she spoke that Yvette had two in her trunk.

As they went up the stairs to get themselves ready for the drive, Kelda put her arm round Yvette's waist and whispered in her ear:

"You were absolutely splendid!"

"I felt like throwing a plate at his head!" Yvette said bitterly.

"Yes, I know. So did I," Kelda agreed. "But you realise that at least we shall be outside the house, and there may be an opportunity for Rémy to get in touch with you."

Yvette gave a deep sigh, then said:

"Supposing he thinks it is—hopeless and does not—try to communicate with me?"

"He will, if it is at all possible," Kelda answered. "I am much more afraid he will do something stupid, like challenging your uncle to a duel!"

Yvette's eyes sparkled for a moment at the idea, then she said:

"You forget that Rémy is a Diplomat and is well aware that he must not do—anything which would cause an— international incident."

They hurriedly put on the hats which matched their gowns and Yvette lent Kelda a sunshade, then they went downstairs again to find Lord Orsett waiting for them in the Hall.

The new curricle, which was drawn by two horses, was large enough to accommodate three people in comfort and a groom sat up behind.

They drove out through the wrought-iron gates with Lord Orsett handling his horses with an expertise that Kelda was sure was exceptional.

She knew that Yvette was looking about her curiously and was aware that it was in the hope that, by some miracle, she might have a chance of seeing Rémy.

As they descended from the high ground and had a glimpse of white sandy beaches and a profusion of flowering shrubs and coconut-trees growing right down to the sea, Kelda exclaimed effusively at the beauty of what she saw.

This was partly to prevent Lord Orsett from noticing that Yvette had nothing enthusiastic or complimentary to say and also because she herself was genuinely entranced by the loveliness of Dakar.

There were only a few large civic buildings in the town, but there were a number that were nearly completed and it was obvious that the Squares, like the roads leading to them, had been planned with the intention of their being decorative.

There were trees in bloom and flowers which made huge patches of colour against the white buildings.

Because Kelda was so attentive, Lord Orsett pointed out to her the Palais de Justice, after which he explained to her the plans that were being made to extend the town.

They saw the flower-vendors who held up their wares as they passed the market and had an original way of balancing a number of their bouquets in their turbans.

"What a charming idea!" Kelda exclaimed.

"It is something which is unique to Dakar," Lord Orsett explained, "and I often wonder who thought of it first."

"She should have a statue erected to her memory," Kelda suggested, and he replied:

"There are plenty of men who feel they should go down to posterity in such a way first."

"But even here in Africa you think women are important," Kelda said challengingly.

She thought for a moment that there was a faint smile at the corner of his firm lips, as if he realised that she was being deliberately provocative.

"I am sure women are important everywhere in the world."

It was an evasion; at the same time, Kelda thought she had forced him to consider what he should reply, and she felt that in some way she had scored a point over him.

When they returned to the house she thanked him profusely for the drive and Yvette echoed it saying:

"It was very interesting, Uncle Maximus, and I do hope we can go driving with you again tomorrow."

"I hope you will not be too tired after we have been riding," he replied.

They walked up the long flight of steps into the front Hall, and he drew his gold watch from his waistcoat pocket. Glancing at it, he said:

"You will wish to tidy yourselves or perhaps change before His Excellency arrives."

"Yes, of course, Uncle Maximus," Yvette agreed. "Where shall we find you when we come downstairs?"

"A servant will tell you where I am," Lord Orsett replied and walked away in the direction of his special Study.

Yvette and Kelda went up the stairs in silence. Only when they reached their own rooms did Yvette say almost frantically:

"What am I to say to the Governor-General? Supposing he tells Rémy that I have agreed to marry him?"

"I do not believe he will ask you to do so in a point-blank manner the first time you meet," Kelda replied. "I may be wrong, and you know far more about Frenchmen than I do, but to me it would seem rather gauche and definitely impolite."

"You are right," Yvette said. "He will merely pay me compliments and insinuate a great many things which I can pretend not to understand."

Kelda thought for a moment.

"Look young and innocent, even rather stupid if you like," she said. "That is what he will expect anyway from anyone of your age, and even if he should suggest it, do not be alone with him."

"No, of course not! You must not leave me! Promise you will not—leave me!"

"I promise," Kelda answered. "But I am sure His Excellency will behave in a very civilised manner, so there is no need for you to feel frightened."

"If only I could see Rémy," Yvette murmured. "How can I learn what he is thinking or feeling at this moment? Suppose he thinks I shall give in to Uncle Maximus?"

"You know he will not believe that, whatever he is told," Kelda said. "Stop being faint-hearted, Yvette. If you are to escape from this dreadful situation, we have to keep our wits about us every minute of the day."

"Oh, Kelda! Kelda! What would I do without you?" Yvette cried. "Thank God you are with me!"

Kelda, as she put her arms round Yvette, also thought it was a good thing that they were together.

She did not underestimate the task she had set herself in saving Yvette, and she thought this morning when they were out driving that Lord Orsett was even more formidable than he had seemed when they had first met.

There was something about him which made her feel he was a conqueror, a man who would always get his own way, a man who would fight to the death rather than surrender!

But it was something she had no intention of saying to Yvette.

Before going downstairs they both changed into elegant gowns which could only have come from Paris.

Yvette's was pale oyster-coloured lace over chiffon with a coral sash round her tiny waist and a coral ribbon round her throat. A very attractive locket set with diamonds which had belonged to her mother hung from a chain round her neck.

She looked very smart and very lovely; and only because she had insisted on it, Kelda was wearing an equally elegant gown of fine silk trimmed with lace that accentuated the blue of her eyes and made her skin seem almost dazzlingly white.

"I would rather be inconspicuous and remain in the background," Kelda had protested when Yvette took it out of her wardrobe.

"You know you cannot do that and have Uncle Maximus concentrating on me with eyes like a hawk! You have to distract him and keep him interested so that I can think about Rémy and watch for him."

"You must not do that too obviously," Kelda said quickly.

"How can I—help it?" Yvette asked with a little sob. "I feel as if five centuries have passed since I last saw him."

A servant led them into an even more magnificent Reception-Room than the one they had used previously. It was, Kelda felt sure, kept for the most formal occasions.

It was not only the decor which she admired but the beautiful arrangements of flowers everywhere that scented the air with their fragrance.

They had no sooner joined Lord Orsett than a servant opened the door and he hurriedly went from the room.

"Where has he gone?" Yvette asked in surprise.

"I think," Kelda replied, "that it is correct for him to meet the Governor-General at the front door."

Yvette came a little nearer to her.

"I am trembling, Kelda. I know it is stupid of me, but I am frightened—frightened that you will not be able to—save me—and in the end I shall have to do what Uncle Maximus—wants and marry this— terrible old man."

"You are not to think like that," Kelda said.

"You have to believe that you will win. Trust in your faith and love. Say a little prayer in your heart and you will feel better and more confident."

"I am praying—I am praying all the time to St. Jude, who is the Patron Saint of lost causes."

"This one is not lost!" Kelda said almost savagely. "But go on praying, Yvette, we need all the Saints on our side."

There was the sound of voices outside the door and a moment later Lord Orsett came in accompanied by the Governor-General.

He was, Kelda thought, exactly how she had pictured him: short, thin, and wiry, with an intelligent face deeply lined with age from spending long years in the tropics. His thinning hair was already turning from grey to white.

After they were introduced to him and they had talked, she realised that he had a certain charm as well as excellent good manners.

But he was old, there was no doubt of that. Old and, to Yvette, terrifying.

She, however, behaved in an exemplary manner so that no-one, not even Lord Orsett, could have found fault. Although she did not say very much, she listened wide-eyed to what was said to her.

She accepted the compliments paid her by the Governor-General with a shy modesty that made him think she had never received any compliments before, and she said charming things about Dakar which undoubtedly pleased both him and Lord Orsett.

Again, it was a performance which Kelda thought might have graced the Comédie-Française.

Only she was aware that Yvette was trembling as she linked her fingers together in her lap so tightly that the knuckles showed white, and every now and then there was a little throb in her voice as if her real feelings might overcome her.

The Governor-General did not stay very long.

Only when he rose to go did he hold Yvette's hand longer than was necessary, and say:

"It has been a great pleasure to meet you, *Mademoiselle* de Villon, and as I wish you to see the Palace, your uncle has promised to bring you and your friend to dinner tonight. It is an occasion to which I shall be looking forward with more pleasure than it is possible to express in mere words."

"I shall look forward to it too," Yvette replied.

There was a sudden light in her eyes which the Governor-General could have been excused for thinking was due to what he had said, but actually Kelda was aware that at the Palace there might be a chance of seeing Rémy.

Lord Orsett escorted His Excellency to his carriage, and when he came back into the room he stood for a moment looking at Yvette and Kelda standing at the other end of it.

There was something searching in his expression, and Kelda noted perceptively that his eyes were a little cynical, as if he questioned to himself whether it was possible that things could be going as smoothly as they appeared to be.

"Am I to understand that you are really looking forward to dining at the Palace this evening?" he enquired.

"Of course," Yvette replied. "I have heard it is a very impressive building."

"Who told you that?"

The question was sharp and Yvette was quick enough to realise what answer her uncle expected her to give.

She looked at Kelda with a puzzled expression.

"Who was it who told us about the Palace, Kelda?" she asked. "Was it the Captain, or those kind people who chaperoned us?"

Kelda was as quick as she was.

"It was the Captain," she said. "His Excellency received him after one of his voyages and it was a gesture he much appreciated."

The suspicion died out of Lord Orsett's eyes.

"I expect after luncheon you would both like to

rest so as to look your best for the festivities this evening," he said. "But in case, Yvette, you are thinking of renewing your acquaintance with the gentleman you met during your voyage here, let me tell you that I have had his name deleted from the list of those who will be presented to you."

For a moment there was an ominous silence, and because she was desperately afraid of what Yvette might say Kelda stepped sideways, and as she did so she knocked over a small table which stood beside one of the chairs.

It fell to the ground with a crash, spilling over an ash-tray and several small ornaments which had been placed on it.

"Oh dear, how clumsy of me!" she exclaimed. "I had not realised it was there. I do hope nothing is broken."

"No, everything is intact," Yvette said, picking up the things from the floor and putting them back on the table.

The moment of danger was passed and Kelda drew a sigh of relief.

Only when after luncheon they went to their rooms did Yvette burst out into a tirade of fury against her uncle.

"How dare he prevent Rémy from coming to the dinner-party! What do you think he said to the Governor-General? What explanation would he give? Perhaps he has ruined Rémy's career!" she cried.

"It is much better that he should not be there," Kelda said quietly.

"What do you mean by that?" Yvette asked almost fiercely.

"If he was, you would have eyes only for him, and all our pretence and your play-acting would be swept away the first moment your uncle saw you together. He would not then believe for one moment that you will agree to marry His Excellency."

Yvette was still for a moment before she said:

"I see what you mean."

"But you will be under the same roof as Rémy," Kelda said, "and I cannot believe that this will not be his opportunity to communicate with us in some way. Be prepared for anything—a whispered word, something thrust into your hand. I do not know what it will be, but I am sure Rémy will take advantage of the fact that you will be there in the Palace."

"I hope so—I do hope so!" Yvette murmured.

The pain in her eyes made Kelda wish she could hurt Lord Orsett in the same manner and he could suffer as he was making his niece suffer.

The gowns she and Yvette wore that evening made Kelda think they were far more suitable for a London Ball than what Yvette called "darkest Africa."

Lord Orsett, looking extremely elegant in his evening-clothes, drove with Yvette and Kelda in a closed carriage to the Palace, which was as impressive as Rémy had told them it was.

A huge building, very much more African in its design than Lord Orsett's mansion, it had a dignity which was enhanced by the soldiers in their short-sleeved red tunics and pointed red hats.

There were only six other guests besides themselves, all of them men, and each was the head of some distinguished Office of State.

It was therefore a party of ten which sat down in the large and impressive Dining-Room and were served with superlative French cuisine, under the direction, Kelda learnt, of a Chef who had come from France and was now training native Chefs to carry on when he returned to Paris.

Because they were the guests of honour Yvette sat on the Governor-General's right and Kelda on his left, while Lord Orsett was entertained by the Minister of Justice at the other end of the table.

Kelda was aware that nothing Yvette did escaped his attention.

She sent her several warning glances during the dinner when she appeared to be looking round as if

Rémy might be concealed in some corner of the room or she might see him through one of the windows.

Because Kelda felt it was important to keep the Governor-General interested, and unaware of the tension from which Yvette was suffering, she made every effort to draw him out about Senegal and found that it was not a difficult thing to do.

He was a man who obviously had a real desire to do his best for the country and for the French Administration of it.

He told Kelda a great many things she wished to hear, and at the end of the dinner she felt that he had been unaware that Yvette had answered him in little more than monosyllables.

In the French manner, there was no question of the ladies leaving the room first, and they all moved together back to the large Salon in which they had been received when they first arrived.

Kelda had forgotten that this was the French custom, although she now remembered her mother mentioning it once many years ago.

It was disappointing because she had half-hoped that if she and Yvette were alone, it might give Rémy an opportunity of joining them. But now there was no chance of that, and it was with a feeling of relief after they had talked for a little while in the Salon that Lord Orsett suggested he should take them home.

"It has been a delightful evening," he said to the Governor-General, "and do not forget that you have promised to dine with us tomorrow night. We shall be greatly looking forward to it."

"Not as much as I am, My Lord," the Governor-General replied.

He looked at Yvette as he spoke and Kelda felt her heart give a frightened throb.

She knew, without being told in words, in fact she was sure, that tomorrow the Governor-General would be given a chance of talking to Yvette alone.

They walked out into the Hall and servants were waiting with the light gauze scarves with which they had covered their shoulders on the way to the Palace.

Kelda waited for the man to help her with hers, turning her back to him so that he should do so. Then as she felt the wrap put round her, she also felt something hard and square being pressed into her hand.

Automatically she closed her fingers over it and a moment later slipped it into the little satin bag she carried, which Yvette had lent her to go with the gown.

Once they had arrived back at Lord Orsett's house, Kelda waited impatiently for him to say goodnight.

"The horses will be at the front door at seven o'clock tomorrow morning," he said. "It is a little later than I usually ride because I would not wish you to ride too far and be stiff, being unable to take much exercise on board ship."

The way he said it made Kelda feel that he wanted to add: "before tonight when your prospective husband is coming to dinner."

But he did not say any more and Yvette replied automatically:

"It will be pleasant to ride again, and you can show us what it is like outside the town, which is very much more sophisticated than I expected."

"I am delighted it pleases you," Lord Orsett said.

He said good-night in a perfunctory manner to Kelda, and as she walked up the stairs beside Yvette she knew how depressed and disappointed the French girl was feeling.

She had hoped against hope to meet Rémy but nothing had happened and they had come away from the Palace without seeing him or without him communicating with them as far as she was aware.

Only when they had reached their bedrooms and the maids had helped them out of their gowns and they were ready for bed could Kelda carry the little satin bag into Yvette's room.

She was lying back against her pillows, an expression of despair on her face until Kelda said:

"Look what I have brought you!"

She held out the bag as she spoke and for a moment Yvette did not understand.

Then she gave a cry.

"You mean . . . ?"

"Open it and see."

"Oh, Kelda, I thought he had forgotten me!"

"See what he has to say, or would you rather read it alone?"

"No, no, of course not! I have no secrets from you."

Yvette pulled open the bag with fingers which seemed clumsy, as if they would not obey her will.

She took out a small square of folded paper on which Rémy had written in very small writing.

Yvette read it through while Kelda waited. Then she said in a voice that was very moving:

"He loves me! He loves me and nothing else matters!"

"What else does he say?" Kelda asked.

"He says we must run away together. He has heard, as you expected, not from the Governor-General but from his Aides-de-Camp, what His Excellency and Uncle Maximus's plans are. He is horrified and says that he will save me, or die in the attempt!"

Yvette gave a little sigh.

"Could any man be more wonderful?"

"What does he suggest?" Kelda enquired.

"He says he is making plans and will tell me about them perhaps tomorrow or the next day. He says someone will give me some flowers and I must handle them carefully because there will be a note hidden inside them."

"Does he say how you can get away," Kelda asked, "and where you can go?"

Yvette was reading the rest of the letter with a rapt expression on her face. After a moment she answered in a very low voice:

"He says he loves me! I am his! He will kill any man who tries to take me away from him! Oh, Kelda, he loves me as I love him and somehow my prayers will be answered and I shall be Rémy's wife."

Yvette and Kelda talked late into the night, and when Yvette had read Rémy's letter a dozen times she passed it to Kelda, who knew from the passionate way he wrote that he was deeply disturbed by what he had learnt when he reached the Palace.

At the same time, she thought, he was man enough not to show his fears or his apprehension to Yvette.

In fact he tried to reassure her, to make her trust him and believe that everything would come right in the end, even though they might encounter many difficulties in the meantime.

"Why did I not think of taking a letter to him?" Yvette asked angrily.

"Because it would have been a very dangerous and very silly thing to do," Kelda replied. "We have no idea which of the servants we could trust in the Palace, and if you had written an indiscreet letter, it might have been handed to the Governor-General, then to your uncle, and we should certainly be watched and guarded more carefully in the future than we are at the moment."

"I suppose you are right," Yvette said in a small voice, "but supposing Rémy thinks I no longer love him?"

"I think he trusts you as you have trusted him," Kelda answered, "and I have a feeling, and it is a very comforting one, that we can leave all the planning that has to be done to Rémy. All we have to do is to carry out his instructions when we receive them."

"He is so wonderful," Yvette said again for the hundredth time.

Kelda was more relieved than Yvette was.

It had been a terrible responsibility planning what Yvette should do and how she should behave, feeling that because she had to take the initiative, if they failed it would be her fault.

Now she was only too thankful to rely on a man, and because she both liked and admired Rémy and he was in fact much older than either of them, she was sure he would be successful in saving Yvette even though the odds were stacked against them.

It was, however, difficult to sleep, and all Kelda could do was try to think of how Rémy could get Yvette away from Lord Orsett's house and how they could escape first from Dakar and then from Senegal without being marched back by soldiers under the command of the Governor-General.

It was all a ghastly puzzle to which there appeared to be no solution.

Even when eventually Kelda fell asleep, she was restless and had dreams in which she and Yvette were being pursued by mysterious figures wearing masks like those which hung on Lord Orsett's walls.

* * *

They were ready in the morning at precisely the time Lord Orsett had said he would be waiting for them and they set off to ride beyond the grounds of the house to where there was no road and it was soft and sandy underfoot.

For the first time Kelda saw strange, round, thatched houses where natives lived and the baobab-trees which were leafless all the year round and had huge trunks and tortured, contorted branches.

They gave Kelda the impression of being the victims of some terrible curse, frozen forever at the instant of punishment.

Where there were a number of them standing together she felt they had a menacing air.

But there were other trees that were full of light and were very beautiful: the great silk-cotton-trees, palms, slender coconuts and bamboos, and there were the fruit-trees she had expected to find in Senegal: oranges, lemons, papayas, avocados, and guavas.

Browsing amongst them were small gazelles, antelopes, and monkeys which scurried away at their approach, and occasionally when they rode near water she could see a glimpse of some huge hippopotamus.

She found it fascinating and she knew as they turned for home that Lord Orsett was pleased at her enthusiasm.

"What do you think of my country?" he asked Yvette, as she had not spoken.

"*Your* country?" she asked. "You are English, Uncle Maximus."

"It is my adopted land," he said, "and the more I learn about Africa and the more I realise how much there is to learn, the more fascinating I find it."

"Do you intend to settle here for the rest of your life?" Yvette asked.

"I expect so," Lord Orsett replied. "It will be a long time, at any rate, before my book is finished."

"Of course..." she began with a sideways glance.

Kelda knew from the tone of her voice that she intended to be deliberately provocative as she added: "As you are so keen on increasing the white population, I expect you yourself will be getting married."

Kelda felt herself gasp at Yvette's audacity, but she knew it was because she was feeling happy and reassured by Rémy's letter that she was no longer so frightened of her uncle as she had been ever since they arrived.

There was a long pause before Lord Orsett replied. Then he said:

"The idea has certainly occurred to me, but as

I have not been back to England for so long, it
seemed somewhat impractical."

As he spoke, riding at a jog-trot with the girls
on each side of him, he turned his head to look at
Kelda and she met his eyes.

For a moment she ceased to breathe.

Then as if she knew what he was thinking without words, she felt herself give a sudden gasp.

It could not be true! He could not be thinking
what she thought he was thinking, she told herself
as they rode on.

And yet she knew unmistakably what had been
in his mind at that particular moment.

Chapter Five

Seeing the Governor-General draw Yvette to the other side of the long Reception-Room in a somewhat obvious fashion, Kelda knew that this was what they had been expecting.

Lord Orsett continued to talk to her as if nothing unusual was happening and she was aware that she must concentrate on him and answer him intelligently.

She would have been far more apprehensive had she not known that in what was a risky yet clever way Rémy had sent Yvette another note.

When the Governor-General had arrived, Lord Orsett had met him at the front door and brought him into the Reception-Room.

He came in carrying in his hand a magnificent bouquet of orchids which on any other occasion would have been a gift to delight the recipient.

Kelda was aware, however, that Yvette was nervous and apprehensive as to what the evening would produce and was longing irrepressibly for some further communication from Rémy.

Even as the Governor-General advanced towards them at Lord Orsett's side, Kelda remembered that Rémy had told Yvette that somebody would give her flowers and she should handle them carefully.

She had not believed it possible that he would

98

be so daring as to hide a note in the bouquet that the Governor-General was himself presenting to the girl he thought would be his future wife.

Then Kelda told herself that perhaps there was no other way in which it was possible to carry a note secretly into Lord Orsett's household.

She wished she could say something to Yvette and warn her to be careful. Then as the Governor-General greeted Yvette and presented her with the bouquet, Kelda was alert.

"I also have a present for you, Miss Lawrence," he said, and handed her a small box tied with ribbon which she was sure contained chocolates.

"How very kind of you to think of me, Your Excellency."

There was a little pause while the Governor-General looked at Yvette and automatically she said:

"The flowers are lovely! I am very—grateful."

"I will put them in water," Kelda said. "Because they are so beautiful we must make them last as long as possible."

She took the bouquet from Yvette as she spoke.

"A servant can do that," Lord Orsett said.

Kelda smiled at him.

"I confess to having forgotten my handkerchief," she said, "so I will give instructions to the maids when I go upstairs. I know Yvette will want these flowers in her bedroom."

Before Lord Orsett could protest further, she hurried from the Reception-Room and ran across the Hall and up the stairs to her bedroom.

As soon as she had shut the door she searched the bouquet and found that there was a very wide ribbon holding the stems of the orchids together.

It only took her a few seconds to undo it and she discovered as she had expected that there was a piece of paper under it, also wrapped round the stems.

She hastily hid it in her drawer, picked up a handkerchief, and called one of the maids who was outside to put the flowers in water. Then she ran downstairs again, knowing that anything that happened this evening was of little consequence.

All that mattered were the instructions which she was sure were written in the note which the Governor-General had unknowingly delivered.

It was even amusing that all unawares he had been the messenger of love. She longed to tell Yvette what she had discovered but she knew it was too dangerous.

Only when they left the Dining-Room, walking ahead with the gentlemen behind them, did Kelda manage to say to Yvette in a low voice:

"The flowers that His Excellency brought you are exactly what you needed!"

She saw Yvette's eyes light up as she looked at her questioningly, and as she smiled a wordless reply, Kelda saw a radiance sweep over Yvette's face almost like the sun rising over the horizon.

Kelda knew that the knowledge that Rémy's note was waiting upstairs would make it easier for her to play her part when, as she suspected, the Governor-General would declare his intentions and she would have to make some sort of answer to him.

"You asked me about my carvings," Lord Orsett was saying, "and there are two in this room which I think are some of the finest examples I have found anywhere."

As he spoke he walked across to a cabinet in which the carvings were displayed and pointed out the terra-cotta head of a man.

"This is Thirteenth-Century," he said, "and comes from Nigeria."

"It is beautiful!" Kelda exclaimed.

"Do you really think so?" he enquired. "Or are you just saying that because you think it is polite?"

"I am telling the truth," Kelda replied, "and I think the ivory carving is beautiful too."

"That is a pectoral mask," Lord Orsett explained.

Kelda looked at them both for some moments, then she said:

"I would be interested to know who they portrayed, but I suppose as they are so old that it is impossible."

"I imagine it is one of their Chiefs or War Leaders," Lord Orsett replied, "and, like poetry, the carvings are in praise of him."

Kelda looked at him for explanation and he said:

"I thought you might know that the praise-name is the most widely used poetic form in Africa. It is applied not only to gods but to men, animals, and plants."

"How exciting!" Kelda exclaimed and she really meant it.

"I presume you are aware," Lord Orsett said, "that poetry in Africa exists almost exclusively in chanted form, or as a song."

"I did not know that," Kelda replied, "but I can understand the Africans finding it easier to express themselves to music more than in any other way."

She looked at the terra-cotta head again, with its fine features, its thick-lipped mouth, and what she felt had been intelligent eyes when the man on whom it had been modelled had been alive.

Because she was so entranced by its appearance she said almost as if she were speaking to her father:

"Recite me a poem, tell me the sort of praise-name which would have been written about a man like this."

Even as she spoke she thought he was surprised, but obligingly Lord Orsett answered:

"I have recently translated one which was written of the great Zulu Chieftain Shaka, but I will not bore you with more than a few lines."

He paused, then recited in his deep voice:

"He is Shaka, the unshakable,
Thunderer—while sitting, Son of Menzi,
He is the bird that preys on other birds,
The battle-axe that excels over other battle-axes."

"That is fascinating!" Kelda said. "But you say it is very long?"

"It goes on for quite a number of pages in my book," Lord Orsett said with a smile. "*Ijaba*—the hunters' songs—usually take as long as the hunts themselves."

Kelda laughed, then she looked round to see that Yvette was coming towards them from the other end of the room.

She did not look particularly agitated, but Kelda thought the Governor-General had a smile of satisfaction on his lips.

"I think I should be leaving now," he said to Lord Orsett, "but I have plans for a large dinner-party at the Palace the day after tomorrow."

"I am sure that will be delightful," Lord Orsett replied.

Kelda saw the sharp glance he gave Yvette and she was sure that he was wondering whether the dinner-party was to be the occasion at which her engagement to the Governor-General would be announced.

The Governor-General held out his hand to Yvette.

"*Au revoir*, Yvette," he said. "I shall count the hours until we meet again."

Kelda heard the emotion in his voice and also was aware that he had called Yvette by her Christian name for the first time.

What was more, after looking at her for a long moment he raised her hand to his lips.

She realised that Yvette gave a little shiver at the touch of his lips but she thought it was almost imperceptible and hoped that Lord Orsett had not noticed.

The Governor-General then turned to her.

"*Au revoir, Mademoiselle* Lawrence."

"*Au revoir*, Your Excellency, and thank you for your present. It was very kind of you."

"It is my pleasure," the Governor-General said automatically.

He walked from the room with Lord Orsett beside him, and only when they were out of hearing did Yvette ask in a whisper:

"There is a letter from Rémy?"

"Yes," Kelda replied, "it is upstairs in my bedroom."

Although she was afraid that they might be overheard, she asked:

"What did His Excellency say to you?"

"What do you expect he would say?" Yvette replied. "He paid me fulsome compliments and said he hoped we would be very happy together when we were married at the end of the month!"

"What did you reply?"

"I said that it had all been a very great surprise to me, and although I was deeply honoured I hoped he would give me time to become accustomed to the idea of being married, especially to someone so distinguished."

Kelda gave a little laugh.

"That was clever of you."

"I tried to think it was not I who was speaking," Yvette said, "but some woman in a play—a play which *must* end happily."

"It will," Kelda said confidently.

It seemed a long time before they could say good-night to Lord Orsett and go upstairs, but as they did—and Kelda thought it was rather tactless of him —he said to Yvette:

"I understand that you have made my friend His Excellency an extremely happy man. I am delighted that you have seen sense and I must commend you on your behaviour this evening and last night when we dined at the Palace."

"I am relieved that you are pleased with me, Uncle Maximus," Yvette answered demurely.

Kelda suddenly had the idea that Lord Orsett

was going to refer to Rémy and say he was relieved
that what he had called a "shipboard romance" was
finished.

Because she did not dare to trust Yvette's reac-
tions in such circumstances, she said quickly:

"I think, My Lord, as we are both rather tired
and somewhat stiff from riding this morning, it
would be wise for us to get our beauty-sleep."

"I am sure you are right, Miss Lawrence," Lord
Orsett replied. "Good-night."

"Good-night, My Lord."

"Good-night, Yvette," Lord Orsett said. "And I
think you are growing to appreciate the attractive-
ness of Senegal. As it is to be your future home,
there is a great deal more I want to show you. Perhaps tomorrow morning you will feel well enough to
ride a little farther than we did today."

"That would be delightful," Yvette answered.
"Good-night, Uncle Maximus."

She turned away with an eagerness that was
irrepressible, and because she was moving so fast
Kelda slipped her arm through hers to force her to
go more slowly.

She had a feeling that Lord Orsett might be more
perceptive than they gave him credit for, and he
might remember and think it strange that she had
taken Yvette's bouquet from the room herself rather
than order a servant to do so.

"Careful!" she warned Yvette under her breath,
and said aloud:

"I personally am feeling very stiff. You will have
to help me up the stairs as if I were an old woman."

"It will wear off by tomorrow morning," Yvette
said.

"I hope so," Kelda replied.

They were both aware that Lord Orsett could
hear what they were saying, but they did not look
back and continued slowly up the stairs and along
the corridor which led to their rooms.

The maids were waiting for them and Yvette had

to be patient until finally they had withdrawn and she was alone.

Then she ran through the communicating doorway to Kelda's room to ask:

"Where is it? Show me! Quickly, quickly! I shall go mad if I have to wait one second more!"

"I know what you are feeling," Kelda replied, "but, dearest, you must be careful."

She opened her drawer and found the letter where she had hidden it, and put it into Yvette's hand.

"Oh, Rémy, Rémy, I love you!" Yvette cried, and kissed the paper before she opened it.

She flung herself down on Kelda's bed, and when she had read only half of what Rémy had written, she looked up, her eyes shining like stars, to say:

"Tomorrow! We are leaving tomorrow!"

"I cannot believe it!" Kelda gasped. "But how? Tell me how!"

"It is all here," Yvette said. "Let me read it to you."

She sat up, holding the letter in her hand, and for a moment she seemed so excited that it was impossible to translate into words what her eyes read.

Then she began:

"I love you, my dearest heart, and I know that it is imperative that we leave immediately before things become more involved and more difficult than they are at the moment.

I am well aware that I am taking a grave risk in sending this letter with the flowers that His Excellency will carry to you personally.

The only servant I can trust in the whole place has the task of arranging them for you and he has told me it would not be safe to try to bribe anyone in His Lordship's household. There is nothing I can do, therefore, except pray that this will reach you.

What I have arranged, and everything de-

pends on you, is that we shall leave Dakar early tomorrow morning in an English ship which is travelling directly from here to Cape Town.

We shall be safe once we get aboard because the French will have no jurisdiction over an English ship. We can be married at sea by the Captain, then you will be my wife. And as it will be a long time before we find our way back to France, it will be impossible for Lord Orsett, or anyone else, to undo what has actually been done."

Yvette gave a little sigh of happiness.

"What he means is that it will be impossible for them to say the marriage is null and void because I have not had my Guardian's permission. And by that time I might easily be having a baby."

Kelda was surprised at the way she reasoned it out, but she waited for the next part of the letter, wondering how Rémy was going to arrange Yvette's departure from the house.

"He then writes a lot of very lovely things," Yvette went on, "about what he will feel once we are married, but this is the important part. . . ."

She read on:

"As I have ascertained, for as you can imagine everything one does is known in Dakar, your uncle goes riding every morning, and today you and Kelda went with him. Tomorrow he will doubtless leave at the same time, seven o'clock, but you must be unwell and Kelda will go with him alone.

The very moment they have left, and from some place of concealment I shall be watching them ride away, I will arrive at the house with a carriage to tell the Head-Servant that the Governor-General has been informed that one of your relatives is dangerously ill and you have to leave immediately for France.

You must be absolutely ready and join me the moment I step into the Hall. We will then rush to the quay and board the ship a few minutes before she sails at seven-thirty."

Kelda gave a little gasp and Yvette said:

"Can anyone be as clever as Rémy? You do see that the servants will be too bemused to do anything but what he says? And we shall be far away from Dakar before you and Uncle Maximus return."

"It sounds as if it might work," Kelda said. "What about clothes?"

"Clothes!" Yvette exclaimed.

Then she threw up her hands, saying:

"Of course! Rémy has forgotten about them! How can I go to Cape Town with nothing but what I stand up in?"

Kelda did not reply and after a moment she said:

"But nothing matters. I will go naked if it means I can marry Rémy and never see the Governor-General or Uncle Maximus again."

"Wait a minute," Kelda said. "I have an idea."

"What is it?"

"We can hardly ask for a trunk to be brought to our rooms. That would certainly seem strange and your uncle might be told about it, but there is nothing to stop you from being extremely unconventional and taking your clothes with you wrapped up in sheets."

Yvette stared at her for a moment in a bewildered fashion, then she gave a little cry of joy.

"Oh, Kelda! Kelda! You are so clever! Of course I can do that! The servants will think it strange, but it does not matter what they think. We will have everything ready here, and just as Rémy is watching you ride away from the outside of the house, I will watch from the inside. Then I will make the maids carry down the bundles and we will take them with us in the carriage."

Kelda and Yvette rose to their feet, then Kelda had another idea.

"We have to convince Lord Orsett that you are not well enough to go riding. It would therefore be wisest that you should be in bed when the maid comes to call you. So we must use my sheets and not yours."

"Do you really think they would tell Uncle Maximus if they thought I was pretending to be ill or tired?"

"It would certainly be taking chances," Kelda said. "You have no idea whether or not he is spying on you, and it would be a mistake to underestimate his intelligence."

She paused for a moment, concentrating with a little frown between her eyes, before she said:

"He is certainly surprised at your being so sensible, and since that first night you have made no mention of Rémy even though you said you were engaged to him."

"We have been banking on his not knowing much about women," Yvette said.

"He is still a very intelligent man," Kelda answered. "He is not as suspicious as he was, but I cannot believe that he does not think it slightly curious that you have accepted the Governor-General's proposal without a protest, without even suggesting the marriage should be delayed for a month or so."

"I see what you mean," Yvette said. "Perhaps that was a mistake."

"Now it is immaterial one way or the other," Kelda went on. "At the same time, you must not put a foot wrong. The maids will call us as they have every morning at half-past-six, and only I will be already up. You will take no notice when they draw back the curtains, and I will go downstairs and tell your uncle how tired you feel and that you would rather spend the morning in bed."

"We will have to make do with your two sheets instead of four," Yvette said in a practical manner.

It took a long time to place all Yvette's most expensive and attractive gowns in the sheets and fasten them with safety-pins so that they could be carried easily to the carriage and from the carriage to the ship.

When there was no room for anything else, they decided they could use also the bottom sheet on Yvette's bed.

In this they packed her hats and sunshades. A pillow-case was filled with her shoes, and when everything was complete the huge white bundles were hidden in Kelda's wardrobe.

Yvette flung her arms round Kelda's neck to say:

"Thank you, thank you! Oh, dearest Kelda, if I really get away tomorrow, I shall be eternally grateful to you for the rest of my life!"

"You have to get away!" Kelda said. "If this fails, I am sure you will never have another opportunity of escaping."

"I know," Yvette said, "and for the rest of the night I shall be praying."

She went to the window as she spoke and looked up at the stars in the sky as if she were already speaking to God, invoking His help.

"I know one thing, Kelda," she said, "that if Rémy and I have to be married by the Captain of an English ship, we will, as soon as we reach Cape Town, find a Catholic Church in which we can be married according to our own religion."

"I feel sure that Rémy has thought of that already," Kelda said with a smile.

"He thinks of everything," Yvette said. "Are you surprised that I am so overwhelmingly in love with him?"

"I think he is very clever and you are very clever too," Kelda replied, "and when he is Prime Minister of France you will obviously make him just the sort of wife a Prime Minister should have."

They both laughed a little tremulously, but their tears were very near the surface.

Then Yvette hugged Kelda again, and because

they both knew it would be wise to rest before the excitement of tomorrow, they went to bed.

*   *   *

It was impossible to lie still, knowing that everything depended on Rémy's planning and on there being no setbacks at the last moment.

She had the terrifying feeling that quite unexpectedly Lord Orsett might decide not to ride this morning, or that because Yvette would not accompany them, she and Rémy would be delayed in leaving the house and the ship would sail before they could reach the quay.

There were hundreds of things that could happen and Kelda found it impossible to lie still. So she rose and dressed herself in the attractive thin riding-habit that Yvette had lent her and put her hat, whip, and gloves ready on the bed.

At six o'clock she went into Yvette's room to find her, as she had expected, half-dressed.

"If I lie under the bed-clothes when the maid comes in," she explained, "she will not be aware what I am wearing."

"My maid usually knocks at my door first," Kelda said, "so I can prevent yours from pulling back the curtains, and tell her that you wish to go on sleeping."

"Suppose they tell Uncle Maximus and he then decides not to go riding?"

"Yes, of course you are right," Kelda said. "We must behave quite normally. Tell her that you just feel sleepy, and let her put out your things for you as usual."

As soon as she spoke she gave a cry of horror.

"I had forgotten your wardrobe is empty! Oh, Yvette, we must think of everything! If we make a mistake now, we are lost!"

"I have already thought of that," Yvette said,

"and as you see my riding-habit is on the chair and I have put what I shall wear in the wardrobe and locked the doors to be quite certain she cannot open them."

"You are cleverer than I am," Kelda said humbly. "My only excuse is that I have not had so many clothes to worry about as you have in the past."

"You will be glad to know that I am leaving you still more," Yvette said. "And after all you have done for me, when you join me in Paris I will give you the most wonderful gowns any girl has ever possessed."

"When do you think you will be in Paris?" Kelda enquired, and Yvette, hearing the serious tone of her voice, said:

"I know, dearest Kelda, you are thinking that Uncle Maximus may send you back immediately to London in disgrace. Here is all the money I brought with me, which is enough to take you to Paris."

She paused, then went on:

"As Rémy suggested, when you get there you must go to my aunt's house and wait for me. I shall write to her and post the letter the moment we arrive in Cape Town, to tell her what has happened. But here, in the meantime, is a note which will introduce you and say how important you are to me."

"How can you think of me at a time like this?" Kelda asked.

"Of course I think of you, because I love you," Yvette replied. "If it had not been for you and the clever way you have made me act a part in front of Uncle Maximus, I am sure by this time I should have been incarcerated in a dungeon or locked up in an attic where Rémy could not reach me!"

"I would not wish to be a . . . burden or a . . . nuisance to you!" Kelda said.

"You will never be that," Yvette said. "Rémy and I will look after you, and one thing I promise, you will never go back to that horrible old Dragon in the Seminary to be bullied as you were before we came here!"

The tears ran down Kelda's cheeks as she kissed Yvette. Then as if she realised that the only thing that mattered at the moment was for Yvette to be ready when Rémy came for her, they both took up what Kelda called their "battle-stations."

Everything went smoothly; the maid came into the room to pull back the curtains, and Yvette said in a sleepy voice:

"I will not get up for the moment. I will call you when I wish to do so."

The maid left the room, having put a tray containing coffee and a warm brioche beside the bed.

Kelda had the same and she carried her cup of coffee into Yvette's room.

"You had better eat something and drink your coffee," she said, "otherwise you may feel faint."

Yvette smiled.

"Not if I know I am going to see Rémy. In fact, I already feel as if I have drunk a whole bottle of champagne and am floating towards the sky."

"You may feel like that, but only when the ship has actually moved out of port," Kelda said, laughing.

She finished dressing, kissed Yvette good-bye, then at exactly ten minutes to seven she walked from her bedroom and spoke to the maids who were waiting in the corridor.

"*Mademoiselle* is fatigued this morning." she said, "and has decided not to go riding. But please listen, for when she calls for you she will require your assistance."

She spoke slowly so that they would understand exactly what she wanted, then went downstairs.

She and Yvette had already carried the large bundles of clothes into her room and set them ready by the door, and Yvette herself was dressed in her travelling-gown, waiting for the moment when Lord Orsett and Kelda rode away from the front door.

This, Kelda knew, was the crucial moment when she must explain to Lord Orsett that his niece would not be joining them but that she herself would like to go riding.

She knew that he, like they, had only coffee in the morning before he went riding, and yesterday they had all had breakfast on the terrace when they returned.

She had no idea where he might be, but when she reached the Hall she saw, with a feeling of relief, through the open door the horses coming round from the stables.

Then along the corridor which led to Lord Orsett's private room she heard footsteps and a moment later he appeared.

If she had not been so agitated and her heart had not been beating so frantically in her breast, she would have thought, as she had yesterday, that he looked exceedingly elegant in his riding-clothes.

All she could think of, however, was the part she had to play and that one slip might ruin Yvette's life.

"Good-morning, Miss Lawrence," Lord Orsett said.

She thought he sounded as if he was in a good temper, perhaps because Yvette had been so charming to the Governor-General last night and had not opposed his plans.

"Good-morning, My Lord," Kelda replied. "I am sorry to tell you that Yvette hopes you will excuse her from riding this morning."

"She is not ill?"

"No, not ill," Kelda replied, "but tired and, as you anticipated, somewhat stiff. She will join us for breakfast when we return, unless of course you would rather I did not accompany you."

As she spoke, she had the feeling that just because she had suggested he should ride alone, he would take the opposite view.

"I see no reason why you should be deprived of your exercise," Lord Orsett said almost immediately.

Kelda hoped the relief she felt did not show too obviously in her face.

"I would like to come," she said, "because you promised to take us on a different ride from where we went yesterday, and I hope that means I shall see some more wild animals."

"We may see some," Lord Orsett replied, "but I had intended this morning to show you both a Bush village and one in particular which I think you will find extremely interesting because it is where the natives dye the fabrics you have already admired."

"I would love that!" Kelda exclaimed. "Oh, please, let us go there."

Lord Orsett smiled and she thought he was amused by her excitement.

It was still not seven o'clock when they walked down the steps and mounted the horses waiting for them outside.

Kelda was sure that somewhere hidden amongst the massive shrubs and trees Rémy was watching them go, and she wished she could wave to him and somehow express her joy that his plan was succeeding.

Instead she merely rode off as quickly as she dared and they were soon out of sight of the house.

It was a glorious morning and the wind from the sea fanned Kelda's cheeks as they rode over the sandy soil.

She tried not to think of what was happening once they had left, and forced herself when they were moving a little slower to draw out Lord Orsett on the subjects in which he was most interested, which were of course Africa and his book.

She found that this was not difficult and she started off by saying:

"I was thinking last night of the magic which everybody seems to associate with Africa. Have you found much of it in your researches?"

"Naturally in primitive people superstitions and what they call 'magic' play a large part in their lives," Lord Orsett replied, "but after I had gone to bed, I remembered an incantation which I thought would interest you."

"Do recite it to me," Kelda begged.

"An *Ibo* diviner, for example, invokes truth before consulting his bones," Lord Orsett explained, "and this one I think is a particularly fine poetical effort. . . ."

He raised his chin a little as if he were looking at the unknown as he recited:

> *"What will it be today?*
> *Success or failure? Death or life?*
> *What is the evil spirit that throws his shade*
> *Between me and the truth?"*

"I like that!" Kelda exclaimed, feeling somehow that it was particularly applicable to what was happening at this moment, and wondering if in some obscure or perceptive manner Lord Orsett, although he was not aware of it, had sensed that something strange was happening.

"At the end of this incantation," he said, "are two lines which I think are particularly poetical:

> *"Here the sun rises—*
> *See the truth come riding on the rays of the sun."*

"That is lovely," Kelda agreed.

There was silence for a moment. Then she said:

"I shall look forward to reading your book."

"The first volume is practically finished."

Kelda looked at him questioningly and there was a faint smile on his lips as he said:

"If you would not find it too difficult to read from the manuscript, then I will give it to you."

"I would love that," Kelda said sincerely.

Then she remembered that once they returned to the house there would be no question of her reading his manuscript or in fact of being there longer than it took to pack her possessions and be sent away on the first available ship.

The idea was depressing because in the short time she had been in Dakar she had seen so little of the countryside and the people.

Thinking how much she would miss, she rode in silence and was therefore startled when Lord Orsett asked:

"What is worrying you?"

Kelda looked at him in surprise.

"H-how do you know I am . . . worried?"

"I am not quite as obtuse and insensitive as you appear to think I am."

For one terrifying moment Kelda thought he was going to say that he had known all along of their plans for Yvette to escape and she was at this moment locked in her bedroom with no chance of reaching Rémy.

Instead he went on:

"I think you are an unusually sensitive person, Miss Lawrence. Sensitive people throw out an inescapable aura that can be picked up by those who are attuned to it. I know, therefore, that something is disturbing you."

"If it is," Kelda replied, "it is not worth thinking about in such beautiful surroundings."

She forged ahead as she spoke, then exclaimed:

"Look, I am sure that is the Bush village! I can see the pointed tops of the roofs."

"You are quite right," Lord Orsett agreed. "At the same time, I hope you will tell me of your trouble or worries, whatever they may be, on the way home."

Because Kelda found so many fascinating things

to see in the village and because she dreaded the revelations that were waiting for Lord Orsett when they returned to the house, she managed to spend a long time not only inspecting the dyeing of the fabrics but also hearing some music.

A tall, broad-shouldered young man played for her and Lord Orsett a *Cora*, the large round calabash acting as sounding-board, with strings made with twisted nerve-fibres.

It made a clear, rather subtle sound which Kelda knew could make a perfect background for the chants or as part of an orchestra for dancers.

"The next thing you and Yvette must see," Lord Orsett said as they rode home, "is the dancing. In Senegal to dance expresses every aspect of life and the dancers wear round their ankles little bells or tiny rattles made of millet-seeds wrapped in leaves."

"It sounds fascinating."

She could not prevent her voice from sounding wistful, because she knew she would leave Dakar without ever having seen the dancers and they would be only something to imagine, in the future, just as in the past years she had had to imagine everything in her life that was beautiful.

Because she thought she would be seeing everything for the last time, she looked round her as they rode home, trying to miss nothing of the trees, the flowers, the fruits, the animals, and the people themselves.

Plodding between the villages were the women carrying large bundles on their heads, and there were men working in the fields, using wooden implements that Kelda was certain went back into antiquity.

Then at last there was the sea and, silhouetted against the sky, the roof of Lord Orsett's house.

Now Kelda's heart began to beat in an agonising manner. Her lips felt dry and it was difficult to respond to anything Lord Orsett said to her.

Two grooms were waiting outside the front door and they went to the heads of the horses as Lord

Orsett dismounted, then moved towards Kelda to help her to the ground.

She had already lifted her leg from the pommel and slipped down, wishing, as she walked up the steps, that the ground would open and swallow her up.

In the Hall she saw waiting beside the servants the elderly man who had met them at the ship on their arrival.

"Good-morning, Bonnier," Lord Orsett said.

Kelda had the idea that there was a slight air of surprise in his voice that he was there.

"I have to inform Your Lordship," *Monsieur* Bonnier said, "that soon after you left, a carriage arrived from the Palace with a message from His Excellency informing us that one of *Mademoiselle*'s relatives was seriously ill in Paris and that she must leave at once, on a ship that was sailing from Dakar this morning at seven-thirty."

As *Monsieur* Bonnier had begun to speak, Lord Orsett had stood still, listening to him, and almost as if she had been ordered to do so Kelda listened too, unable to move away.

"*Mademoiselle* caught the ship?" Lord Orsett asked after a pause.

"I understand so, M'Lord. She had already left when I was informed of what had happened."

"Who came from the Palace to collect her?"

Kelda drew in her breath.

"I do not know his name, My Lord," *Monsieur* Bonnier replied, "but he was a young man and I think he is one of the Equerries in attendance upon His Excellency."

Lord Orsett's lips tightened, and now for the first time since *Monsieur* Bonnier had begun to speak he looked at Kelda.

"I wish to speak to you, Miss Lawrence," he said, and there was a note in his voice that made her shiver.

He walked across the Hall and she followed him.

He opened the door of the room into which they had been shown when they first arrived.

She followed him into it, the door was shut behind her, and he turned round to face her.

"You were aware that this would happen," he said sharply. "I require an explanation."

For a moment Kelda thought it was absolutely impossible for her to speak.

Then in a voice that she meant to be calm and unhurried but which in fact sounded frightened, she replied:

"You could not be so ... foolish as to believe that loving ... Rémy Mendès as ... Yvette does, and he her ... they would tamely submit to your plans for her to ... m-marry somebody else."

"Who planned this, and how?" Lord Orsett demanded angrily.

"Does it matter?" Kelda asked. "They are to be married without your consent, and I do not think there is much you can do about it."

"I can have the ship stopped at St. Louis," Lord Orsett said furiously, "or at any rate when they reach Marseilles I will make sure that this man is arrested for abducting a minor."

He spoke so angrily that his voice seemed to echo from wall to wall.

"And how will that help Yvette ... if by that time she is ... having a child?" Kelda asked.

She saw by his expression that this had not occurred to Lord Orsett.

Then with a muttered exclamation which might have been an oath, he turned and walked away towards one of the windows.

He stood for a moment looking out to sea. Because in a way she could understand what he was feeling now that his plans had gone awry, Kelda said hesitatingly:

"I am . . . sorry if you are . . . angry . . . but love
. . . real love . . . cannot be . . . suppressed or f-forgotten
overnight . . . as you seem to . . . think it . . . can."

Lord Orsett did not move or speak, and after a
moment Kelda went on:

"Yvette will be happy . . . and because she is such
a sweet and attractive person . . . surely you want her
happiness?"

Still there was no response from Lord Orsett,
until in a voice that was harsh with anger he said:

"Go upstairs and change! I shall expect you
to be ready to accompany me in twenty minutes!"

Kelda wanted to ask him why and where they
were going, but she was too frightened.

Instead she opened the door, hurried into the
Hall, and ran up the stairs.

Only as she reached the top step did she hear
Lord Orsett calling for *Monsieur* Bonnier.

'Perhaps he is making arrangements to send me
home,' she thought, and felt her spirits sinking into
a depression that was almost like falling into a deep,
dark hole.

'If I have to go I shall be alone again,' she
thought, 'and although Rémy and Yvette have been
so kind, there is nowhere I belong . . . nowhere where
I would feel as I have felt here . . . happy.'

She reached the top of the staircase and looked
back to see *Monsieur* Bonnier hurrying in answer
to Lord Orsett's call.

"What is to happen to me?" Kelda asked herself.

She knew despairingly that once again, as when
her father and mother had died, her world had
come to an end and there was nothing left but
insecurity and fear.

Chapter Six

Kelda went slowly down the stairs, feeling as if every footstep was an effort.

The maid had had ready her bath, which she always had after riding, and as she lay in its scented water she recalled how difficult it had been to wash adequately at the Seminary.

There were baths for the pupils, but when she wanted one she had to use an ancient bathroom that had not been painted for years and which led off the kitchen.

All the water had to be heated on the stove and carried in cans which were almost too heavy for her to lift.

The only alternative was to wash in cold water and to dry herself on the small, inadequate, often ragged towels which Mrs. Gladwin thought were good enough for her.

To be able to wash in comfort, to be waited on, and to have her gowns pressed every time she wore them were joys that she appreciated more and more every day that she stayed in Lord Orsett's house.

Now, she told herself, this would come to an end, together with all the other pleasures she had enjoyed, and she would leave Senegal with only the memory of its beauty to cherish for the rest of her life.

Through the open front door she could see the flaming red of a hibiscus-blossom and beyond, clambering in exotic profusion by the gates, a riot of purple bougainvillaea.

She had felt ever since she came to Dakar that the colours of the flowers warmed her as the sun did, and when she thought of the January cold in England she shivered.

With her eyes wide and frightened she walked into the Salon where she expected Lord Orsett would be waiting.

He was standing at the far end of the room and she felt as she walked towards him that she might be covering miles, instead of feet, to reach him.

She could hardly bear to look at him, knowing there would be a scowl between his eyes and he would still be as angry as he had been when she left him.

She drew nearer and still nearer, until when she stood still he said in a harsh voice which did not surprise her:

"I have decided to offer you a choice."

At his words Kelda glanced at him quickly, saw as she had expected the grimness of his face, and looked away again.

"Choice?" she questioned, finding it difficult to speak.

"You have connived with my niece to circumvent the plans which I had made with a great deal of forethought," he said, "and I can now take you either to the Palace or to the Palais de Justice."

Kelda started and there was silence before she asked in a voice that trembled:

"You . . . would have me . . . put in . . . p-prison?"

"You might consider it that," Lord Orsett replied, "but as it happens, I am suggesting that you will either take my niece's place and marry the Governor-General, or marry me!"

Kelda gave a frightened gasp, then without thinking what she was saying she exclaimed:

"You must be mad!"

"Merely practical," Lord Orsett replied. "I brought Yvette out here for a special purpose, and since you have both seen fit to flout my authority and take matters into your own hands, you are left to make reparation for her behaviour."

"It is ... impossible that you can ... really mean that I should .. marry the Governor-General ... or you!"

"That is exactly what I do mean," Lord Orsett said. "As I have already explained, it is important for the future of Dakar that there should be more European women here in a predominately male society, and as you qualify for the position—the choice is yours!"

"Do you really ... think I would ... accept such a ... suggestion or agree to marry in such ... circumstances?"

"I am afraid you have no alternative," Lord Orsett said drily, "but if you need any encouragement to do what I wish, then you may feel more inclined to acquiesce without unnecessary fuss if I concede, on your agreeing, not to prosecute this young man who you have decided is an eminently suitable husband for my niece."

Kelda drew in her breath.

She realised that Lord Orsett was making it quite impossible for her to refuse his suggestion of marriage.

At the same time, every nerve in her body, every instinct within her, told her that this was as outrageous and diabolical for her as it had been for Yvette.

How could she contemplate being married to a man like the Governor-General, who was not only old but until now had thought of her only as the companion to the woman he really wished to take as his wife?

As for Lord Orsett . . .

Her thoughts stopped suddenly.

It occurred to her almost insidiously, as if someone were speaking in her ear, that here was her opportunity to remain in Dakar, to stay with the sunshine and the flowers, to be no longer afraid of an unknown future either in France or in England.

She would be safe, at least from the stigma of being a "Charity Child," which she had carried for so long that she felt it was branded upon her brow.

The picture of being secure seemed to flash before her eyes.

She felt as if instinctively she held out her arms to it, but she knew that such security involved accepting Lord Orsett himself, who was angry with her because she had helped Yvette to escape and more frightening and overwhelming than she had imagined any man could be.

His voice broke in on her thoughts.

"Well? Have you made up your mind?" he asked. "I imagine you would find your position as wife of the Governor-General influential and important enough to compensate for any other shortcomings he may have."

She knew that Lord Orsett was sneering at her with that cynical note in his voice which she found more frightening than when he raged in anger.

She clasped her hands together and found that they were cold and trembling.

"Do I . . . really have to . . . make a . . . choice?" she asked in a voice barely above a whisper.

"Alternatively, you can leave and return to England, and I will deal with young Mendès in a way he richly deserves!"

From the manner in which he spoke, Kelda knew it was no use appealing to Lord Orsett for mercy or understanding.

She had thought when she first saw him that he was a conqueror, a man who always got his own way, a man who would win over any opposition by sheer force of character.

If he said he would punish Rémy, he would certainly do so, and she knew it would be unthinkable for her to destroy both his and Yvette's happiness.

Moreover, although perhaps it was a selfish idea, she knew that if they were parted, if Lord Orsett should be instrumental in sending Rémy to prison, then there would be no place for her in Paris.

In which case she must go back to the Seminary and endure the life of servitude she had lived before she came to Senegal.

As if he was impatient for a decision, Lord Orsett drew a watch from his waistcoat pocket and looked at it. Then as he replaced it, Kelda said in a voice that was barely audible:

"I ... I will ... m-marry you!"

"You are sure that is what you want?" Lord Orsett enquired.

Kelda drew in her breath.

"There is ... first something I must tell you ... then I think you will no ... longer wish to m-marry me ... and the Governor-General would certainly not accept me as his ... wife."

She thought Lord Orsett looked surprised.

She walked away from where she had been standing, facing him, to one of the windows to stare out with unseeing eyes on the glittering beauty of the sea and the vivid colours of the flowers below the terrace.

Because she felt it almost unbearably humiliating to tell Lord Orsett what she knew he must hear, she held on to the window-sill, pressing her fingers against the wood.

She stood there for what seemed a long time before Lord Orsett's voice behind her said:

"I am waiting."

"I am not . . . what I . . . appear to be," Kelda began, forcing her voice from her lips with an effort. "I . . . came here ostensibly as Yvette's f-friend and companion, but I was . . . really sent in a very . . . different . . . capacity."

She felt, although he did not say anything, that Lord Orsett was surprised at what she had said, and she thought, although she was not certain, that he came a little nearer to her.

"When . . . my father and mother were . . . killed in an earthquake in Turkey," Kelda went on, "I was sent first to an . . . Orphanage. I was a . . . 'Charity Child.'"

She could not help a little sob escaping from her lips as she said the words which had been flung at her derisively for so long and which still hurt when she had to say them herself.

"I was there for three years," she continued. "Then at fifteen I was sent as a . . . servant to Mrs. Gladwin's Seminary for Young Ladies."

"A servant?" Lord Orsett questioned, as if he thought he could not have heard the word correctly.

"A maid of all work, a maid who did everything that nobody else was willing to do," Kelda answered. "I scrubbed the floors . . . I washed the dishes . . . I was at the beck and call of the other servants."

She thought Lord Orsett was too astonished to speak, and because she knew she had to finish the story, she continued quickly:

"Two years ago I was promoted to waiting on the mistresses . . . to helping the pupils in the School with their clothes and their mending."

For some reason which she could not explain, she wanted to be completely honest, and she added:

"I deliberately sought to ingratiate myself with Yvette de Villon because I wished to . . . improve my French. She became fond of me . . . and offered me her friendship."

She turned to face Lord Orsett and stood silhouetted in the sunshine coming through the window.

"When you ... sent for Yvette, nobody else would come out to Africa with her. The mistresses all refused, so I was told to accompany her, act as her lady's-maid on the voyage ... and to return ... if possible ... by the next ship."

Although she had turned round, she hardly dared to look at Lord Orsett's face.

She stole a quick glance at him and thought he was not scowling as deeply as he had before.

"Whose idea was it," he asked, "that you should pose as Yvette's friend and wear her clothes?"

"I was dressed in the ... drab grey garments which were identical with what I had ... worn in the ... Orphanage," Kelda explained, "and it was Rémy Mendès who thought I could ... help them to convince you that he and Yvette should be married ... if I were ... properly dressed."

"So you expected opposition from me and intended to deceive me even before you reached Africa?"

"Yvette thought you would not ... agree to her marriage because she was ... so young. She never dreamt in her wildest imaginings that you had planned to marry her off to an ... old man whom she had never ... seen."

"Most women would consider it an advantageous marriage from a social point of view," Lord Orsett said drily.

"B-but Yvette was ... in love."

"While for you that question does not arise."

"Do you really think any Frenchman," Kelda asked, "and they are all, I believe, exceedingly snobbish from the highest to the lowest, would wish to take a ... 'Charity Child' as his wife?"

"We are not, as it happens, discussing how the French feel," Lord Orsett said. "You have already said that you would prefer to marry me."

"How can you ... of all people ... marry a ... woman who has ... spent the last eight years of her life in circumstances which must make anyone in the Social World spurn her as if she were a leper?" Kelda asked with an angry note in her voice.

She felt that Lord Orsett was deliberately torturing her.

She had told him the truth, and now he was dangling in front of her eyes the position she might have occupied if she had continued to deceive him and had not been so honest.

As if he guessed what her thoughts were, he said:

"You need not have told me this."

"But supposing you had ... found out afterwards? Supposing the newspapers discovered and revealed the life your wife had lived before she became ... a lady?"

Kelda sighed.

"I have told you the truth ... and now I suppose you will make arrangements for me to ... leave as soon as there is a ... ship sailing to Europe."

"So you wish to go back to England?"

Kelda almost cried out that that was the last thing she wanted to do, now or ever.

Again because she thought it was right that she should be honest, she said:

"Yvette and Rémy said they would ... find me a position in Paris if I would ... join them there."

"Doing what?"

The question was sharp.

"Rémy Mendès has three sisters. He was sure one of them would want me to teach her children English."

"So you would prefer to be a Governess who has to accept the crumbs from a rich man's table rather than stay here and marry me!"

There was silence as Kelda stared at him.

"Are you saying," she asked after a moment,

"that ... after what I have told you ... after you know the truth about me ... you would still ... marry me?"

"I dislike my plans being upset," Lord Orsett said as if in explanation. "If you are ready, we will drive to the Palais de Justice, where, because *La Mairie* is not yet completed, weddings take place before the Mayor, as is compulsory under the law in France."

Kelda stared at him incredulously.

"You are ... sure that what you are ... doing ... is right?"

"That is what I wish to do," Lord Orsett replied loftily.

She was astonished into silence. There was nothing she could say, nothing she felt she could do.

She thought it could not be true and she must be dreaming that she was to be married to a man who she felt regarded her not only with anger but with distaste.

But what could she do about it?

She could not allow him to prosecute Rémy, and even if there was a chance of her running away, where could she go?

He walked across the room and as he opened the door she passed him with her head down, too afraid to look at the expression she would see on his face.

An open carriage with a white awning was waiting outside the front door.

Kelda stepped into it and only as they drove away from the house did she think that never in her wildest dreams had she thought that she would marry in Dakar, or in such circumstances.

When she had seen Yvette and Rémy together, so much in love and utterly content with each other, she had involuntarily said a little prayer in her heart that one day she might find love.

She knew it was something she craved because since her father and mother had died nobody had loved her, and nobody except Yvette had even had the slightest affection for her.

She knew instinctively that there was something within herself that could be expressed in no other way but by love.

She knew that beauty, which she found in music, in the books she read, and in the flowers that were so abundant in Senegal, was part of an emotion that reached out from her, waiting to give love and to receive it.

Now without love she was to be married, and she felt as if an icy hand took her heart and squeezed it so that it was hard to breathe.

"I am to be married!" her mind told her.

Yet it was impossible to realise that it was actually happening and was not something she had imagined. Woman-like, she glanced down to see if what she was wearing was appropriate for the occasion.

When she was changing she had been so frightened by Lord Orsett's anger that she could think of nothing but what he might do to punish her. So she had not chosen what gown she would wear, but had left it to her maid.

Now she saw that it was one of Yvette's favourites, a very pretty pink with a sash in a deeper hue that was echoed by the roses that trimmed her small straw hat.

It was in fact, if she could not wear white, the perfect choice for a bride on what should be the most perfect day of her life.

But to Kelda pink was the colour of love and for her on this her wedding-day there was no love, only fear and apprehension.

They reached the Palais de Justice and Kelda saw *Monsieur* Bonnier waiting for them outside the impressive front door.

It struck her that Lord Orsett must have sent him on ahead to make arrangements, and she was surprised that he had been so sure that her choice of husband—even before he knew the shadow over her background—would be himself.

He had spoken as if he were certain that she would choose the position of wife to the Governor-General. Yet there was *Monsieur* Bonnier waiting, and as they stepped out of the carriage she heard him say to Lord Orsett:

"Everything is arranged, M'Lord. The Mayor is waiting to receive you."

They were escorted by an official who bowed very low to Lord Orsett along a number of corridors to a part of the Palais that was not concerned with the Law Courts.

The official opened the door and announced:

"Lord Orsett, *Monsieur le Maire!*"

An elderly Frenchman, wearing the elaborate and picturesque uniform of his position, rose from behind a large desk with a genial smile on his face.

* * *

Driving back to the house, Kelda was acutely conscious that Lord Orsett had, since they had made their responses to the Mayor and been united as man and wife, not addressed one word to her any more than he had spoken on their drive into the town.

She felt she should say something but felt tongue-tied because she was shy.

She was married! She was Lord Orsett's wife! It was too incredible to contemplate, let alone talk about.

It could not be true that after eight years of misery and humiliation, after being derided continuously and found fault with by Mrs. Gladwin, she was now in a position which would be envied by any of the girls in the School.

In fact, Kelda thought, they would be only too willing to change places with her.

She had heard them so often talk of their own futures and always they had been concerned with marrying a man who was aristocratic and rich.

It had never seemed to her that love entered into their calculations, although they simpered and giggled at the compliments they had been paid during the holidays from the young men who tried to steal a kiss.

But where husbands were concerned it was a very different matter and they all appeared to have a very clear idea of what social position they wanted to occupy in the future.

In many cases they even accepted with surprising complacency the idea that their marriage would be arranged entirely between their parents and the parents of the intended bridegroom.

Kelda had listened with only half an ear to what they were saying, for her mind was usually preoccupied with what she was learning from the books she borrowed.

Now the memory of things that had been said came back to her, and she was sure that she had made a marriage of which any mother of a pupil in the Seminary would have approved.

"But I want ... love," she told herself, then thought she was being too demanding.

She should be grateful, deeply grateful, that there was now no question of her having to return to London and Mrs. Gladwin, or to Paris to accept what Lord Orsett had described as "the crumbs from a rich man's table."

At the same time, because the silent man sitting beside her was her husband, she felt her heart pounding in her breast and her lips felt dry to the point where it was impossible to speak.

As the carriage reached the iron gates and passed through them, Kelda thought that the flowers of the crimson hibiscus were even more vivid against the white of the building than they had been when she had left.

'This is my home,' she thought, 'something I have not had since I was a child.'

"We will have luncheon immediately," Lord Orsett said as the carriage drew to a standstill outside the front door. "I imagine that as you had no breakfast this morning you must be feeling quite hungry."

He spoke in such an ordinary, conversational voice that it was easy for Kelda to reply:

"Yes ... I am ... now that I think about it ... very hungry, My Lord."

As she spoke, she wondered if, now that they were married, she should address him as "My Lord," and knew she would be far too shy and embarrassed to speak to him in any other way.

Because she had no wish to keep him waiting, she took off her hat in the Hall and gave it to one of the servants, and without bothering further about her appearance she just patted her hair into place and stood waiting to see where Lord Orsett would wish to go.

"A bottle of champagne!" she heard him say to the head-servant. "And inform the Chef that we require luncheon at once."

He then walked towards the terrace and Kelda followed him.

The sun was now shining so brilliantly on the dancing waves that it was almost blinding. There was the pervasive fragrance of the flowers and the soft trade wind blew away the oppressive heat.

She felt a sudden excitement seep over her, almost as if she had already drunk the champagne.

She did not have to leave!

She could stay here, she could go on looking at the beauty all round her, she need no longer feel afraid of everything she said, because there was no more need for secrecy, no more need to be careful.

She stood looking at the scene as if she were seeing it all for the first time, then was aware that Lord Orsett had seated himself at a table under one of the awnings and was watching her.

She turned towards him impulsively.

"It is so lovely!"

She knew it was something she had said a dozen times to him before when they had been riding, when they had looked at his native carvings, and in fact whenever they spoke of anything to do with Senegal.

Now it was more poignant and the exclamation came from her very soul because the loveliness had become a part of her and she belonged to it.

He did not reply as the servants appeared with the champagne. They poured out two glasses of the golden wine, then Lord Orsett lifted his as if in a toast to Kelda.

"To our future!" he said, and his words surprised her.

"I . . . I hope I may . . . make you . . . h-happy," she said hesitatingly after pausing to think what she should say.

Even as she spoke she thought it was very unlikely.

She had the feeling that he would never be happy. His cynicism and perhaps his hatred were too deeply ingrained in him.

Then she told herself she would have to try.

It was what her mother would have expected her to do, and yet she felt helplessly inadequate for the task.

What did she know about men? Certainly nothing about a man as self-sufficient as Lord Orsett. What preparation had she for the life she was to lead now?

Humbly she told herself she was completely the wrong person for him to have married, and she was convinced that the only reason he had done so was because he could not bear to be proved wrong.

He could not allow his cherished plan to fall to bits completely and have to start all over again to find a woman who would come out to live in Dakar.

She thought he would also feel humiliated in having to explain to the Governor-General that Yvette

had not only run away rather than marry him but
that one of his own staff had actually connived in
the operation.

The situation was extremely uncomfortable for
Lord Orsett and Kelda found herself feeling quite
sorry for him.

"Luncheon is served!" one of the servants announced, and she thought he was about to say something but instead he set down his glass and rose to
his feet.

They walked down the corridor towards the
Dining-Room together.

Because Kelda remembered that her mother had
always thought it extremely bad manners for people
to sit during meals saying nothing, she forced herself, because there were servants in the room, to
speak of ordinary things.

"You will not forget," she said, "that you promised I might see the manuscript of your book?"

They were talking in English and those waiting
on them would not understand what was said. At the
same time, they would know they were conversing
amicably.

"I have not forgotten," Lord Orsett replied.

"How did you start your momentous task of writing a history?"

"I started by reading about Africa," he answered.
"I read how the Phoenicians came here, then the
Greeks, followed by the Romans, the Vandals, the
Byzantines, then the first Muslims."

"It sounds fascinating, but very hard work."

"It is."

"I have always heard that the Muslim religion
has a very mystical side to it."

"I see you know more than I expected," Lord
Orsett said, "and you will therefore appreciate what
I have written."

"It will be very exciting for ... me."

They went on talking about the different peo-
ples who inhabited Africa.

She thought as they talked that he appeared to have forgotten his anger, and because she was really interested in what he was saying she plied him with questions and forgot for a moment that there was a strange relationship between them.

She talked to him as if to a man who could tell her so much that she wanted to know, which indeed he could.

After coffee had been served and Lord Orsett had accepted a glass of brandy, the servants withdrew.

For the first time since they had sat down at the meal Kelda felt constrained and shy.

It struck her that there were so many questions she wanted to ask about their future life together, and yet she had no idea how to begin.

She had the feeling that he too was considering his words and perhaps something else, but she could not guess what it might be.

She only felt apprehensively that he was thinking of her and she longed to know in what way.

Then suddenly the door opened and a woman came into the room.

For a moment, because she was wearing native dress, Kelda thought she must be a servant and barely glanced at her.

Then as she realised that Lord Orsett had stiffened to attention, she looked again and saw the woman was extremely attractive and, she was sure, a *métisse*.

There was no mistaking the distinct trace of European in her features. At the same time, her smooth coffee-coloured skin spoke of her African ancestry.

She carried herself superbly and her hair was arranged in the individual hair-style of a dozen tiny plaits curled round at the end, which was characteristic, as Kelda had already seen, of many of the native women in Dakar.

She wore a *boubous* in an exquisite shade of

purple and her gold jewellery interspersed with amber was obviously very valuable. She walked towards the table with an unmistakable self-assurance, her eyes on Lord Orsett.

"What do you want, Antoinette?" he enquired in French.

"I have been told in the market," the woman replied, speaking in the same language, "that you are married. I cannot believe it is true or that you would not have informed me of it before the ceremony actually took place."

"I intended doing that this afternoon."

As Antoinette opened her mouth to speak again, he rose to his feet.

"As you are here," he said, "we can talk about it now in another room."

He walked towards the door as he spoke, opened it, and went out without waiting for her.

She followed him without even glancing in Kelda's direction, and it was impossible not to notice that she moved with an exquisite grace that was somehow reminiscent of the gazelles that Kelda had seen when she had been out riding.

Kelda sat at the dining-room table as if she had turned to stone.

So this was the woman Yvette had heard one of her cousins speaking about and whom he had said was a *métisse*.

There was no doubt that that was what she was, and she thought she could understand what Lord Orsett felt about her, because she was extremely beautiful and as vivid as the flowers outside.

A quarter-of-an-hour went by and now the excitement Kelda had felt before luncheon, the joy of feeling safe, secure, and belonging, had gone.

Instead, she felt a sudden depression sweep over her almost as if the sunshine were blotted out.

In response to Lord Orsett's toast she had replied that she hoped she would make him happy, but now she felt that there was no reason for her to trouble herself on his account when he had Antoinette.

It struck her how hollow her life would be when all he required of her was that she should be simply an instrument to persuade other women, principally French, to come out and live in Dakar.

There was nothing she personally could do for him. She was just a symbol, and doubtless he would find it more and more irksome even to pretend to enjoy her company.

All these years, she told herself, while he had gained the reputation of being a recluse, he had found contentment in writing his book and with Antoinette.

Kelda thought how inadequate her own looks must appear beside those of the *métisse*.

Antoinette was tall, with that superb carriage of those who for generations had walked with heavy loads upon their heads. She would also, because of her mixed blood, Kelda thought, have the fascination and the *joie de vivre* which had been so characteristic of Yvette.

She had always felt that the French had a charm which the English could never emulate, and Antoinette would doubtless have her father's quick wit and her mother's calm acceptance of life which was so characteristic in Africa.

She had also the mystery and the magic of which she and Lord Orsett had just been talking.

Kelda wondered how many years she and Lord Orsett had been together; years in which perhaps he had loved her as she loved him.

But he could not marry her even though he might long to. Perhaps secretly Antoinette had hoped he would do so, only now to have her hopes shattered with the news that he had married somebody else.

Lord Orsett came back into the room.

He seemed unperturbed and moved in an unhurried manner back to his place at the top of the table.

Kelda watched him.

What had he and Antoinette said to each other? What had happened when they were alone?

Lord Orsett seated himself and picked up his glass of brandy.

"I must apologise for that untimely interruption," he said in his usual cynical voice. "Antoinette wanted to make sure of her money and behaved somewhat unconventionally by coming to collect it in person."

The way he spoke, the indifference with which he dismissed the whole episode, made Kelda feel suddenly very angry.

Without really meaning to, she rose to her feet.

"I am sure that is ... untrue!" she said. "I do not know how you can ... speak in such a manner of someone who ... loves you! Although you may not be ... aware of it ... women have hearts!"

Her voice broke on the last word. Then because she could not bear him to see how deeply he had affected her, she turned and ran from the room as swiftly as her feet would carry her along the passage and up the stairs.

One of the maids was at the top of them and when Kelda would have turned in the direction of her bedroom she said:

"This way, Madame."

Kelda, fighting for self-control, was not prepared to argue but allowed the maid to lead her into a large bedroom she had not seen before.

There was a huge four-poster bed draped at the top with white mosquito-netting in a manner which made it appear like a galleon with its sails set.

But Kelda had no eyes for the room. She only wished to be alone.

"Madame must have a *siesta*," the maid said.

Because for the moment she could not trust her voice, Kelda stood still as her pink gown was unbuttoned and taken from her.

Then one of the soft, lace-trimmed nightgowns

that Yvette had given her was put over her head, and almost before she was aware of what was happening she was in bed, the blinds were lowered, and the door closed softly behind the departing maid.

It was then that Kelda put both her hands over her face, and as if the mere action of doing so released the tension within her like the collapse of a dam, she burst into tears.

She cried tempestuously in an abandoned manner as she had not cried since her father and mother had been killed.

She could not really reason to herself why she was so unhappy.

It merely seemed as if once again her world had fallen apart, her dreams were shattered in pieces, and everything she had wished for was smashed and broken.

* * *

Kelda stirred, realised she had been asleep for a long time, and heard somebody moving carefully about the room.

She opened her eyes and knew that when she had got into bed the sun had been hot and golden outside.

Now it was dark.

She thought at first that it was only because the curtains were drawn, then she knew it was night and the maid was lighting the candles on her dressing-table.

"What time is it?" she asked.

"Seven o'clock, Madame, and I have prepared your bath."

"Seven o'clock?" Kelda repeated stupidly.

She knew she had slept not only because she was desperately tired, having had no sleep the night before, but also because of the dramas she had experienced earlier in the day and because she had cried to the point of utter exhaustion.

"I suppose I should get up," she said almost to herself, as if she half-hoped there would be no need and she could stay here alone and not have to see the man who was now her husband.

"Dinner is at eight, Madame," the maid said, "and *Monsieur* does not like to be kept waiting."

The maid's words, spoken in halting French, made Kelda get out of bed.

Her bath was cool and refreshing and she washed her face in cold water in the hope that it would erase any sign of her tears.

Then she told herself that he would not notice anyway after the rude manner in which she had run away, and would have gone in search of Antoinette to console him.

Doubtless they spent their time in the part of the house which was private to him, and he would think how beautiful she was and she would amuse him and make him laugh.

Then Kelda told herself severely that she should not be thinking of Antoinette. That was the secret side of Lord Orsett's life, on which even as his wife she could not encroach.

Now she could understand why he had been content to stay for so long in Africa and not return to England.

His relatives had thought it was just because he was a recluse, but would a man have need of any other companionship when he could have somebody as beautiful as Antoinette as—Kelda made herself face the word—his mistress?

Because she had lived such a cloistered, sheltered life since her father and mother had died, she had not come in contact with men, nor had there been anybody to talk to her about their ways or what they thought and felt about women.

She knew only the snatches of conversation that

she overheard from the giggling school-girls and what she read in the books that she borrowed from the class-rooms and which very seldom dealt with anything to do with love.

What she had learnt in her travelling with her father and mother was very little, but she was aware that the men of many African tribes had four wives and the Sultan of Turkey had a large harem of women.

It had all seemed rather unreal and not translatable into flesh and blood.

But now she had seen Antoinette, and she understood, she thought, that a man would find such a beautiful woman irresistible, and that she should try to compete with her for Lord Orsett's affections was out of the question.

When she had dried herself after her bath and put on the few underclothes it was necessary to wear in the evenings, her maid said:

"As Madame is a bride, she must wear a white gown this evening."

"I do not think I have one," Kelda replied automatically, thinking as she spoke that she felt very unlike a bride and the dark cloud of despair still hung over her.

Her eyes too felt heavy from crying and she knew she had no wish to go downstairs and meet Lord Orsett again, feeling that he would certainly be condemning her for her behaviour.

"What does it matter if he does?" Kelda asked herself crossly. "Everything I have done is wrong to him. He will never really forgive me for helping Yvette to escape, and he made it quite clear that I should marry the Governor-General rather than him."

Nevertheless, when her maid brought from the wardrobe a gown that had been Yvette's, she was mildly interested.

It was a ball-gown of white satin covered in tulle and sprinkled with diamanté, which she now remembered Yvette had said was too voluminous to pack.

"There is no room for it," she had said petulantly when Kelda had pointed out that it was still hanging in the wardrobe. "Besides, I have never liked myself in dead white."

It certainly did not become her so much as the bright colours she usually wore, Kelda thought, but when the maid fastened her into the white gown she knew she looked different from how she had ever looked before.

Wearing the lovely gown and with her shoulders swathed in white tulle, the diamanté sparkled with every move she made. She looked bridal.

The bodice was very tight and her waist looked tiny above the swirling skirts, and the maid arranged her hair in a fashionable style on top of her head; then, looking at her reflection in the glass, she said:

"*Attendez un moment, Madame!*" and ran from the room.

Kelda wondered what she was doing, and when she returned a few seconds later with two white camelias in her hand, she understood.

The maid arranged them on top of her head and it seemed to complete the elegance of the gown, though she knew that Yvette would doubtless have worn diamonds.

"*Madame est très belle!*" the maid exclaimed several times, and Kelda forced a smile in response.

Only as she went downstairs, feeling rather self-conscious, did she wonder if perhaps Lord Orsett would be amused at her for dressing up in such an elaborate manner.

He might even think it pretentious of her when their marriage was so far from normal. As Kelda reached the Hall she had an impulse to run upstairs again and put on one of the gowns she had worn before.

Then as the head-servant came forward she knew she was in fact almost late, since it lacked only a minute or so to eight o'clock and Lord Orsett disliked being kept waiting.

She therefore followed the servant who led her to a Reception-Room where her husband was waiting.

He too looked very elegant in his evening-clothes, Kelda thought, but if he noticed anything strange about her appearance he did not say so.

Instead, as she walked towards him he picked up a glass of champagne from a side-table and gave it into her hand.

"I hear you have been asleep."

"I am ... sorry if it was ... inconvenient."

"It was very sensible," he contradicted. "I realise you had very little sleep last night."

She thought he must be angry because by now the servants would have told him that Yvette had taken most of her clothes with her and had packed them up in his sheets. But he spoke almost as if he was amused and went on:

"There is nothing more fatiguing than dramatic or unexpected situations—at least that is what I have always found."

He was, Kelda thought, trying to dispel any awkwardness which might exist between them due to Antoinette's appearance and her own outburst.

Because it was impossible for her not to be responsive in the circumstances, she said with a wavering little smile:

"I ... I am sorry I could not come ... driving as ... I think ... we planned."

"It was better for you to sleep," Lord Orsett replied, "and you missed accompanying me to the Palace—a visit which was slightly uncomfortable."

He was speaking lightly and Kelda looked at him in surprise.

"His Excellency was extremely disappointed," he said in reply to her unspoken question, "but he congratulated me warmly and wished to give a large dinner in our honour as soon as you feel you can face such a gastronomic exercise."

Kelda gave a little laugh as he had obviously intended her to do, then dinner was announced and they went into the Dining-Room.

As she entered the room Kelda stood still in amazement.

The last thing she had expected was any kind of celebration of their marriage, but the room had been transformed with garlands of white flowers hanging from the walls and great banks of them arranged in the corners of the room.

The table was all white with the same camelias as she was wearing in her hair, and on a table at the far end of the room was a large and elaborate wedding-cake.

It was all so unexpected and at the same time, for someone who had never been given a celebration of any sort in her life, an irrepressible excitement.

"H-how ... could you ... think of it? How could you ... do anything so ... marvellous?" Kelda stammered.

"I hoped you would like it," Lord Orsett said simply.

"Of course I like it!" she replied. "But ... the cake ... how could one have been baked so quickly?"

"I have to admit that was bought, and my Chef has lost face in consequence!" Lord Orsett said with a smile. "But he is determined to hold his own by producing a dinner which, if we eat everything he has prepared, will strain our capacity to its utmost point of endurance!"

Kelda was listening. At the same time she was looking round with the excitement of a child at his first Pantomime.

Flowers scented the room and from the candelabrum entwined with flowers the candles cast a golden light which made everything seem to have a magic she had never known before.

"Y-you did this for ... me? Really ... for me?" she asked beneath her breath, as if she still could not believe that it had not been meant for somebody else.

"I am trying to make up for the somewhat banal Service that took place in front of the Mayor," Lord Orsett replied. "I believe every woman when she is married wants a Cathedral, a choir, and at least ten bridesmaids!"

Kelda gave a little laugh.

"I do not know one person I could ask to be my ... bridesmaid."

As soon as she spoke she thought that that was the sort of wedding Lord Orsett must have had when he had been married to Yvette's aunt.

In thinking of Antoinette she had forgotten that he had been married before and his wife had died.

Had he loved her desperately? she wondered now. Was that perhaps why he looked so cynical and why at first he had shut himself away from the world?

Perhaps then he had sworn he would never love again and had never found a woman who could equal in any way the Frenchwoman who had borne his name.

'If I were French,' Kelda thought miserably, 'perhaps I could make him happy.'

She looked at him quickly from under her dark eye-lashes and thought that no man could look more distinguished or more handsome.

His eyes met hers and there seemed to be a strange expression in them which she did not understand, but she told herself it was because the light from the candelabrum distorted everything.

At the same time, she was aware that her heart was beating in a strange manner, and although she could not quite understand it, the cloud of depression that had hovered over her ever since luncheon was lifting.

Chapter Seven

As the long and elaborate dinner ended, the head-servant, before he withdrew, spoke to Lord Orsett in a low voice, who then nodded and said to Kelda:

"The staff want to wish us happiness, but as they are Moslems they cannot drink our health. I think, therefore, that we should divide the wedding-cake amongst them."

"I am sure they will enjoy it," Kelda agreed.

"And since to placate the Chef we will have to eat the one he is baking tomorrow, we can just cut this one in traditional fashion and let it be taken outside."

Lord Orsett rose from the table as he spoke, and Kelda, knowing it was expected of her, walked to join him at the side-table on which the large wedding-cake was arranged.

It was a typical French confection of white icing with a large silver bell on top and silver horse-shoes and imitation orange-blossoms decorating each of the three tiers.

The head-servant produced a long, sharp knife and handed it to Kelda.

As she took it, looking rather helplessly at the cake and wondering whether she should start with the top tier or the bottom one, Lord Orsett said:

"I think, if we are correct, we should cut it together."

He put his hand over hers as he spoke. At the touch of his fingers and because he was so near to her Kelda felt a strange sensation flash through her.

It was, she thought, half-pleasure and half-pain, and unlike anything she had ever felt before.

It was the first time Lord Orsett had touched her except for the moment when he had placed the wedding-ring on her finger in front of the Mayor.

Then she had been too bemused to be conscious of anything except to think she was dreaming.

Now she was acutely aware of Lord Orsett and the nearness of him.

Guided by his hand, she thrust the knife into the bottom tier of the cake, and when it had cut through to the large silver tray on which it was standing, he said:

"I think we have performed our part. Now it can be taken away and given to those who I hope will enjoy every mouthful."

With an effort, because she was shy at what she was feeling, Kelda enquired:

"I know it would be ... impossible for me to ... eat any more than I have done already."

"I feel the same," Lord Orsett agreed, "so let us go into a Salon. Tonight we will sit in the one at the far end of the house."

Kelda wondered vaguely at his choice, but when she entered the room she saw that it too had been decorated with white flowers, not with the same profusion or with garlands as in the Dining-Room, but there were huge vases on the tables and the scent of lilies filled the room.

"Thank ... you," she said, feeling almost overwhelmed because he had been so thoughtful.

She walked to one of the tables on which there was a beautiful arrangement of camelias and stood looking down at them.

She was aware that Lord Orsett had walked

across the room behind her and was now standing only a few feet away.

"Why have you been crying?" he asked.

Because he spoke so gently and in a voice that was different from any she had heard him use before, she felt the tears come into her eyes again.

'It must be because I am tired,' she thought, but she knew that that was not the reason why she had cried so desperately and despairingly before she fell asleep.

When she did not reply, Lord Orsett said after a moment:

"I have a present for you, for I feel you should have one on your wedding-day."

As he spoke, Kelda saw, almost as if she were looking at a picture, the amber and gold necklace which Antoinette had worn round her neck, and, without considering her words, speaking impulsively, she said quickly:

"I do not . . . want a present. Please . . . do not give me . . . anything!"

She thought Lord Orsett was surprised although she did not turn to look at him, knowing that if she did, he would see the tears which were making it impossible for her to see the camelias.

"Why do you say that?" he asked.

Then after a moment, as if he had found the reason for himself, he said:

"I think I have a lot of explaining to do. Suppose you sit down, Kelda, and listen to me."

He paused for a moment before he added:

"It is important for our future—together."

There was just a pause before he spoke the last word and Kelda drew in her breath.

At least he intended that they should have a future together, even though so much of his life would never be hers.

Obediently, still not looking at him, she moved towards one of the large sofas and sat down in a corner of it.

He chose a chair opposite her and she had the uncomfortable feeling that from there he could watch her face and would know what she was feeling. Because she did not wish him to see too much, she looked down at her hands, which she clasped in her lap.

There was silence and it flashed through Kelda's thoughts that Lord Orsett had changed his mind and would not, after all, explain anything to her.

Then he said very calmly in what she felt was a deliberately impersonal voice:

"You know from Yvette that I was married to her aunt, Ginette de Villon?"

It was a question, but Kelda would not trust herself to speak and merely nodded her head.

"I am sure you must have wondered, and certainly Yvette did, why, having married somebody so attractive who loved the gaieties of Paris, I brought my wife to Dakar and made her stay here until she —died."

There was something in the way Lord Orsett spoke which, even though his tone was quiet and calm, told Kelda he was finding it hard to speak of the past, and she had the feeling that he had not confided in anyone in such a way before.

She thought she might be wrong, until he went on:

"Nobody except my wife was aware of my real reason for coming here, and I have never until this moment revealed it to anyone."

Because she felt embarrassed for him, Kelda said quickly:

"I shall understand ... if you do not wish to ... tell me."

"It is your right to know," Lord Orsett replied, "and I am determined that there should be no secrets between us."

Kelda looked at him in surprise, for it was something she had never expected he would say. Then as he went on she looked down once again at her hands.

"I fell in love with Ginette when I met her in London. I found her fascinating and quite unlike any of the young women I had met at Balls and Receptions who were approved of by my mother as being eminently suitable to be my wife."

Lord Orsett's lips tightened for a moment before he went on:

"It was what was called 'a whirlwind courtship,' and because I was young and very idealistic and inexperienced I did not think it strange that when I first met Ginette she appeared not to take the slightest interest in me, then suddenly, overnight, changed completely and became as much the pursuer as the pursued."

Now there was definitely a bitter cynicism in Lord Orsett's voice and a note too as if he mocked at himself.

"I was too happy to be critical or inquisitive, and the moment we were engaged we went to Paris, where I was accepted effusively by the De Villon family. We were married, had a short honeymoon, then returned to London."

Kelda was listening intently and she knew by the inflections in Lord Orsett's voice how difficult he was finding it to relate what had happened.

"It was some little time before I understood my wife's partiality for London, and also why our marriage had taken place in such haste."

Again he paused.

"No-one actually told me the truth, it was just a look, a laugh, an innuendo, and the fact that when I came into a room there always seemed to be a sudden silence, as if the people in it had been talking about me."

Bitterly he went on:

"My 'Fool's Paradise' did not last long. In the Marlborough House Set, in which we moved, it would have been impossible for anything to remain a secret for long. There were always too many people involved."

Kelda glanced up at him curiously. The lines on his face were deeply etched as if even speaking of what had happened brought back the pain.

"I think I must have been married for two months," Lord Orsett said after a pause, "when I understood the reason for Ginette's eagerness to become my wife."

Because she felt she must know the answer, Kelda asked in a voice just above a whisper:

"What . . . was it?"

"She had met the Prince of Wales, the heir to the throne, in France. She had become infatuated with him, or rather with his position and the aura that surrounded him. She followed him to England, determined to have what she considered the honour of becoming his mistress."

"Oh . . . no!" Kelda murmured.

"The Prince, however, made it clear that he never indulged in love-affairs with unmarried women. All his mistresses were married to complacent husbands. That was the part my wife had assigned to me."

Kelda drew in her breath.

Whatever she had expected to hear, it was not this.

"When I learnt the truth, the whole truth," Lord Orsett said harshly, "I told Ginette that she had been mistaken, that I not only refused to be placed in such an invidious position, but I would not allow anyone who bore my name to disgrace it."

For a moment Lord Orsett's voice seemed to ring out in the flower-scented room. Then he continued more quietly:

"I had heard of Dakar. I was also already interested in Africa, then a little-known part of the world. I brought Ginette, despite her protests, out here—and she died two years later."

His voice seemed to die away into the shadows and there was silence until Kelda said very softly:

"I am . . . sorry. It must have . . . hurt you a great deal."

"I suppose 'hurt' is the right word," Lord Orsett replied. "But it was my pride which suffered most. I could not bear to be sneered at, laughed at behind my back, or subjected to the winks and nudges that other men in the same position endured. When Ginette died, it would have been possible for me to return home but by then I did not want to go back."

"So you . . . stayed to write your . . . book."

"I began my research for it," Lord Orsett corrected. "I travelled all over Africa, meeting different tribes, living with them, learning a great deal about their customs which nobody had ever known before."

"It must have been very . . . exciting."

"I had built this house," Lord Orsett went on, "and when it was finished I found I liked being here and enjoyed the isolation of it. I no longer missed the friends I had known in England. When I wanted companionship there were always intelligent men like the Governor-General to talk to."

He paused.

The word "companionship" made Kelda think of Antoinette, and as if he knew what she was thinking, Lord Orsett said after a moment:

"You have by now realised that the French understand better than the English that a man, whatever his position, needs a woman in his life."

Kelda found it hard to breathe.

Of course Lord Orsett, being so handsome and attractive, had wanted women and they had wanted him.

She could see, almost as if she stood in the room with them, the beauty and grace of Antoinette, the outline of her features, the golden texture of her skin against the purple *boubous* and the jewelled necklace which Lord Orsett must have given her.

Then as once again she knew that feeling of

despair and agony which had made her cry when she had gone upstairs to her bedroom, she felt she could not bear to hear him telling her how much Antoinette meant to him and how even though they were married he could not give her up.

She had a feeling that he would ask her to be sympathetic, to accept the fact that their position as man and wife was not an ordinary one, and to accustom herself to the French way of life.

She remembered now reading about the Kings of France, who always had both a wife and a mistress and that such situations were accepted not only by the Court but by the French nation as a whole.

She felt, however, that she might cry out that she could not bear it, that it was something she could not endure.

To control herself she clasped her fingers with such intensity that they hurt, and she forced herself not to move as Lord Orsett went on:

"Because Dakar, like many other French outposts, is isolated from Europe, and even news of their relatives is delayed in reaching those who live here, the Government and the companies for whom the men work recommend marriage to local women."

He paused.

"Those who do not marry have of course mistresses, and the arrangement, as I told you and Yvette when you arrived, has certain businesslike rules attached to it which are strictly adhered to."

"I remember . . . that," Kelda murmured.

"The *métisses* with their French blood make it easier for the more fastidious men to accept them because many are in fact well educated, while the majority of the natives are completely illiterate."

So Antoinette, Kelda thought, was clever as well as beautiful.

It was what she might have expected where Lord Orsett was concerned, and she thought that perhaps there was nothing original in thinking that she might help him with his book when Antoinette would know a great deal about the local tribes and could be of real assistance to him.

She could doubtless supply every detail he required on all the subjects which interested him, and if he travelled away from Dakar she could go with him.

Kelda thought with dismay that her very last hope of being able to help Lord Orsett lay smashed, as were her other dreams and ideals.

Again, she wanted to say that there was no point in her hearing any more.

He would make it very clear that there was no part for her in his life except as a woman who would sit at the head of his table when he entertained and accompany him on official occasions.

Otherwise she would be alone, while Antoinette shared with him everything that mattered.

She wanted to cry out that it was unfair, that in the circumstances he should never have married her.

The pain she felt was the same pain she had known when she had first been taken to the Orphanage and realised that she no longer had any identity or personality of her own and was just one of a number of faceless, forgotten children.

"What I am explaining to you," Lord Orsett was saying, "is the position Antoinette has occupied in my life."

"I . . . I understand that . . . already," Kelda said quickly.

As she spoke, she felt that she could not bear to hear any more; she did not want to listen to what he had to tell her of what the *métisse* had meant to him and how it would be impossible for him to give her up.

Lord Orsett ignored her interruption and merely said:

"Antoinette had no right to come here today and

I told her so. But she has enough French blood in her to be very shrewd, businesslike, and calculating where money is concerned."

Kelda raised her head wonderingly.

"Antoinette has been with me for three years," Lord Orsett said, "and during that time she has been assiduously accumulating every penny that I have given her, so that as soon as our liaison was over, she could marry another *métisse* who has also been saving so that they can start a shop together."

Now Kelda stared at Lord Orsett in astonishment.

"You mean . . . even while she was . . . with you . . . she wished to . . . marry somebody else?"

"I have told you, these things are well arranged in Dakar and in all French Colonial communities. Antoinette was intelligent enough to know that the one thing she needed was money, and the easiest way to obtain it was to become the mistress of a rich man."

"But . . . she must have . . . loved you?"

"I do not think the word ever occurred to her where I am concerned," Lord Orsett replied. "She found me generous, I provided her with comforts she would not otherwise have had, and she was discreet. That is of course understood in the arrangement between a man and his mistress all the world over."

As if he thought Kelda still did not comprehend what he was saying, he explained:

"It is a mistress's object to get as much from her protector as she can. They both accept that when the arrangement is over there will be no hard feelings, no recriminations. The man pays for the pleasure he has had, but that is all. It finishes without dramatics."

"And . . . Antoinette does not mind . . . losing you?"

The question was barely audible, but Lord Orsett heard it.

"I doubt if she will shed a single tear on my

behalf," he said with a smile. "In fact I would be very much surprised if she is not at this moment celebrating with her young man because the large sum of money I gave her this afternoon will enable their marriage to take place immediately."

"I . . . I do not . . . understand," Kelda said almost to herself.

It was impossible to sit listening to Lord Orsett any longer, and she rose from her seat and walked to the window, pushing aside the curtains so that she could look out.

The window was not closed, and although it was much cooler than it had been during the day, the night air was warm and moist.

Outside, the moonlight was silver on the sea and the sky glittered with stars.

But Kelda was looking into her heart, wondering why the things Lord Orsett had told her seemed suddenly to have melted away the heaviness she had felt, which had grown and grown in her breast until she had been almost stifled by it.

Then as she stood there she felt Lord Orsett close behind her.

"I have made my explanations," he said quietly, "and now I think it is only fair that you should explain two things to me."

"What . . . are . . . they?"

"First, why you have been crying, and secondly why you told me that women have hearts."

Again, because his voice was so quiet and gentle, she found herself too moved to answer him, and after a moment he said:

"That they have hearts was something I thought existed only in romantic fiction. As I have just told you, the women I have known have used me for their own ends. That I am therefore diabolical, as you once said I am, is surely no surprise."

"I am . . . sorry I said . . . that," Kelda murmured. "It is . . . not true."

"Women have hearts," he repeated ruminatingly.

"I would like to see some sign of it. Have you a heart, Kelda?"

"I hope . . . so."

"I meant, of course, where I am concerned. What do you feel about me?"

Kelda felt his question was quite impossible to answer, and as she tried wildly to think of what she should say, Lord Orsett went on:

"I expected you to say that you would marry the Governor-General. After all, his position is far more important than mine. Also he would be likely to die sooner and leave you a rich woman."

"Do you . . . imagine I would . . . think of something like that?"

"Being you, I suppose not," Lord Orsett replied, "but I am sure it is the way most women would think."

"Only the women . . . you have . . . known," Kelda said. "I believe that women want to . . . love a man for . . . himself . . . not for what he can . . . give them."

"And you have known many women like that?"

"Yvette would not marry for money; she would have married Rémy even if he had not a penny to his name."

"And you are like her?"

Kelda did not answer and after a moment he said:

"You have not answered my other question."

"I do not . . . know what you . . . asked," Kelda said almost defiantly.

"You are not very good at lying," Lord Orsett said. "This morning when we were riding together, I knew that something was worrying you and that you were tense and apprehensive. I admit I did not guess the reason, but I knew what you were feeling."

He was right, but Kelda did not admit it, and he continued:

"Then when we drove to our wedding you were frightened, and I could understand that. On the way back your fear gradually faded and at luncheon you were almost happy. I could feel it reaching out towards me as if you felt you had found something for which you had been searching, something which made you feel different from how you had ever felt before."

Kelda was so surprised by what he was saying that she turned round to look at him.

Now in the light both from the candles and the moonlight outside, she saw an expression in his eyes that made her heart start beating furiously and she could not look away.

"But Antoinette came to see me," Lord Orsett said very quietly, "and when I came back into the Dining-Room you were unhappy, and when you told me that women have hearts, your voice broke."

As he spoke he came a step nearer to her, and yet Kelda could not take her eyes from his.

"Then you cried," he went on, "tears which I think came from your heart, a heart that I am quite certain you have, although I would like to think it belongs to me."

Now once again his voice was so gentle and so compelling that Kelda felt the tears well into her eyes, and before she could stop them they ran down her cheeks.

She tried to turn away but Lord Orsett's arms were round her.

"Are those tears for me, Kelda?" he asked. "If so, they are very precious."

She could not answer; she could only hide her face against his shoulder, and he felt her whole body trembling. His lips were against her hair as he said:

"I want your heart, Kelda. I want it more than I have ever wanted anything in my whole life, but I am so afraid, so desperately afraid, of being disillusioned as I have been before."

Because of the pain in his voice and because there was also a hint of fear that Kelda had never expected to hear from him, she was no longer afraid herself.

"Y-you ... want me?" she asked. "You ... really ... want me?"

"It is difficult to tell you how much."

"She is ... so beautiful. I thought I could mean ... nothing ... to you."

Lord Orsett smiled very tenderly.

"I have tried to make you understand why I have not loved anyone for many years, and what I feel for you is different from anything I have ever felt before."

"Is ... that true?"

Kelda was looking up at him. The tears were still on her cheeks, but her eyes were shining and the question seemed to throb not only on her lips but through her whole body.

"I love you!" Lord Orsett said positively. "I have loved you from the moment I saw you, but I told myself it was just another illusion and there was no chance that you would care for me except because I am a rich man."

"How ... could you ... believe that would ... matter?"

He looked down at her, a faint smile on his lips. Then he said:

"Tell me what I want to hear. Say it, my darling!"

The colour rose in her cheeks as she whispered in such a low voice that he could barely hear her:

"I love ... you! I know now that is why I ... cried ... because I thought I had ... lost you ... and you would ... never have any ... use for me."

The last words were lost as Lord Orsett's lips came down on hers, holding her captive.

Then as he kissed her, Kelda knew that this was what she had wanted, what she had cried and longed for.

She felt as if the moon and the stars outside, the fragrance of the flowers round them, and the beauty of the sunshine of Dakar were all in the sensation Lord Orsett's kiss gave her.

At the same time, there was only him and he filled the world and the sky.

He drew her closer and closer and his lips became more demanding, more passionate, and yet Kelda was not afraid.

She thought for one wild moment that if only she could die now she would have known the perfection and glory of love that she thought could never be hers.

Then she knew she wanted to live. She wanted to live for the love she had found with the man who drew her poor, starved, hungry little soul from her body and made it his.

He kissed her until the rapture of it made her feel as if she could no longer think but only feel, as if her whole body vibrated to a wild music that came from God.

Then as Lord Orsett raised his head she gave a little murmur of protest because she could not bear to lose the ecstasy he had given her, and she said incoherently:

"I . . . love you . . . how can I . . . tell you how . . . much I love you?"

"I just want you to go on saying it," he said, "until I believe you and you believe me and there is nothing else of any importance."

"How . . . could there . . . be?" Kelda asked.

Then he was kissing her again.

*   *   *

Kelda stirred and realised, with a feeling of inexpressible happiness running through her, that her head was on her husband's shoulder and the pale dawn sunshine was seeping through the curtains.

She moved a little closer and said, as if she could not believe it:

"You are . . . there!"

"I am here, my darling."

"How ... could I go to ... sleep and ... lose you even for a moment?"

"I was holding you close," he answered, "and you know now that we can never lose each other again."

"Do you ... still love ... me?"

He smiled and kissed her forehead.

"Are you really asking me such a foolish question? But actually it is one I meant to ask you."

"That would be even ... more foolish," Kelda replied. "I did not know it was possible that a man could be so wonderful ... so strong and yet so gentle and ... exciting."

"Did I excite you?"

She thought there was a faint touch of laughter in his voice that she had never heard before.

Because she was shy, she turned her face against his shoulder once again.

"You ... know you ... did."

"Not half as much as I mean to do in the future," he said. "I have so much to teach you, my precious one."

"You know now how ... ignorant I am," Kelda said humbly. "I did not ... do anything ... wrong?"

His arms tightened.

"Everything you did was right, perfect, and more wonderful than I can ever tell you."

"You will ... teach me about ... love?"

"That is something I shall enjoy doing," he replied, "and, my darling, it is love that will teach us both far better than anything else that we belong to each other."

Kelda was silent for a moment, then she said:

"There is ... something I want to ... ask you."

"What is it, my dearest heart?"

"When you ... loved me, it was more ... wonderful than anything I can say in words ... but did you feel ... different from the way you have ... felt with ... other women?"

He smiled very tenderly and put his fingers under her chin to turn her face up to his.

"I shall always tell you the truth," he said, "and this, my beautiful, precious wife, is true: I have never before known such happiness as you gave me last night!"

He spoke very solemnly, but Kelda gave a little cry of sheer delight.

"That is all I wanted you to ... say ... because it means that I can give you ... something which ... nobody else has ... given you."

She paused before she went on:

"I felt yesterday, when I was so unhappy, that once again I had nothing. I was just a ... 'Charity Child.' But if I can give you what ... no-one else can do ... then I am no longer poor and ... insignificant."

"You will never be that again, ever!" Lord Orsett said. "You have a place in my life which is more important, more vital than anything else I possess."

"Do you ... really mean ... that?"

"I swear to you that I mean it and it is true. This is what I have missed! This is what I wanted when I was young and idealistic and thought that I would never find."

Kelda gave a sigh of sheer happiness, then she said:

"You do really ... believe that if you were of no ... importance and you had no money ... no marvellous house, but were just an ordinary man, I should still love you as ... I do now?"

"That is what I want to believe, but I want you to work very hard, my darling love, to convince me."

"I will ... try ... I will really try."

As she spoke, Kelda put out her arm across his chest as if she wanted to reassure herself that he was really there. As if he understood, he said:

"We have many years in which to convince each

other about our love, and while you have been sleeping, I have been making plans."

"What sort of . . . plans?"

"Plans to make you happy," he said, "and what I know will be best for the wife whom I worship and adore."

"What are these . . . plans?"

"Nothing frightening," he said reassuringly. "It is just that I have decided that while we shall stay in Dakar in the winter, we will go to England in the summer."

"Oh . . . no!"

"I think it right that you, and also I, who have sadly neglected my responsibilities in the last few years, should go back to the land of our birth. I will open my house in London, but I think you will be happiest, and I know I will be, on the Estate I have in Leicestershire."

He kissed her hair before he added:

"If nothing else, you will enjoy the horses that I intend to buy and we will ride together over the best hunting-country in England."

Just for a moment Kelda felt frightened. Then she told herself that she must think of Lord Orsett.

He was still a young man and it was a mistake for him to bury himself away from his roots and the people with whom he should associate, and also from his responsibilities in the County to which he belonged.

She felt that in this her mother was guiding her to say the right thing, helping her at this particular moment to know instinctively that it was a crossroads not only in her life but in her husband's.

"Oh, darling," she said with a note of passion in her voice, "wherever we were, I would be happy with . . . you. I will do whatever you want, but you must help me not to make . . . mistakes . . . not to . . . shame you in any . . . way."

She knew Lord Orsett was moved by what she said, but before he could reply she went on:

"I have led such a very different life these last eight years since Mama and Papa died, and I realise how ignorant I shall be of the Social World, the way to behave ... what I should say ... what I should do. But ... if you are there and you will ... teach me, I will not be ... afraid."

"I will never let you be afraid again," Lord Orsett said. "You must forgive me, my darling, for frightening you as I have in so many ways since you came here."

He gave a laugh and said:

"You accused me that very first evening of trying to behave as if I were God. Now you are asking me to go on doing so."

"This is different!" Kelda said. "Because then you were acting with indifference or hatred ... but now you are acting with ... love, and that is what ... God does."

"My precious, you have an answer for everything," Lord Orsett answered, "and I adore your clever little brain, but then I adore everything about you—your face, your very revealing, sensitive eyes, your lips, and of course your body, which is now mine."

His hands moved softly across her skin and Kelda felt the strange fire which he had kindled last night reawaken within her.

She thought vaguely, far away at the back of her mind, that she had read somewhere of the fire of love, but when she felt it, it was different from anything she had imagined.

She knew as it burned within her that what she felt was the ecstasy of love, it was what she had longed for, and it could only be there if two people were joined divinely as one, and was too perfect ever to be described in words.

"How can I tell you how happy I am?" Lord Orsett asked.

"I want you to be so ... happy that you are never ... angry or bitter ... again."

He was kissing her eyes as she added:

"It is strange ... but when I was falling in ... love with you, I kept thinking that you made me feel ... safe and secure, which is something I had ... longed for ... and yet now I want to keep ... you safe and ... protect you from being hurt or ... unhappy."

"That is what you must do, my darling," Lord Orsett replied. "Now that I am so happy, I realise how lonely and miserable I have been in the past. I told myself I was self-sufficient, that I wanted nothing. Then I found you, and I became aware how empty my life had been. Perhaps I have wasted these last years quite unnecessarily."

Because she could not bear him to regret the past, Kelda said quickly:

"I am sure that is not true. The book you have written will be of inestimable benefit to Europeans who want to understand about Africa, and to the Africans themselves."

"I would like to believe that."

"I am sure it will be true, and one day your children will be very proud that they have such a clever father."

Kelda spoke without thinking, then as she realised what she had said, the colour rose in her cheeks and she hid her face against him.

"My children!" Lord Orsett said very quietly. "That is another thing that has been missing in my life."

Once again he turned her face up to his as he said:

"Will you give me a son, my dearest love? I would like him to be born in England in the house where I was born. I would be proud to think I have provided posterity not only with a book about Africa but with a child to carry on my family name."

"I shall ... try very hard ... not only to give you one son but ... several."

"And a daughter as beautiful as you."

"If . . . that is what you . . . want," she replied. "But . . . please . . . do not . . . love any of . . . them more than . . . me."

"I was going to say the same to you," he replied with a smile. "You are mine, Kelda, mine completely and absolutely. I shall be jealous even of my own children if they take all your attention."

"They will never do that," Kelda answered, "because it is so wonderful for me, after having been alone . . . an orphan . . . unwanted, to . . . belong . . . to know that I am secure and . . . safe. I want to stay like this . . . close in your arms, for ever and ever. . . ."

"That is exactly what you will do," Lord Orsett replied. "I have found you, my darling, when I did not believe you even existed, and I will never lose you again—never!"

He looked down at her, and as he did so, she saw the fire growing in his eyes and felt the insistence of his hands against her body.

Then it seemed to her that the flames of the fire within her rose higher and higher until they reached her lips, and she wanted with a yearning that was agonising in its intensity for him to kiss her.

She lifted her mouth, and as he held it captive, she felt as if the room was filled with sunshine, golden and glorious.

Then as his heart beat on hers, she knew that they were "riding on the rays of the sun" into a Heaven that was all their own.

ABOUT THE AUTHOR

BARBARA CARTLAND, the world's most famous romantic novelist, who is also an historian, playwright, lecturer, political speaker and television personality, has now written over 200 books.

She has also had many historical works published and has written four autobiographies as well as the biographies of her mother and that of her brother Ronald Cartland, who was the first Member of Parliament to be killed in the last war. This book has a preface by Sir Winston Churchill.

Barbara Cartland has sold 100 million books over the world, more than half of these in the U.S.A. She broke the world record in 1975 by writing twenty books, and her own record in 1976 with twenty-one. In addition, her album of love songs has just been published, sung with the Royal Philharmonic Orchestra.

In private life, Barbara Cartland, who is a Dame of the Order of St. John of Jerusalem, has fought for better conditions and salaries for Midwives and Nurses. As President of the Royal College of Midwives (Hertfordshire Branch), she has been invested with the first Badge of Office ever given in Great Britain which was subscribed to by the Midwives themselves. She has also championed the cause for old people and founded the first Romany Gypsy Camp in the world.

Barbara Cartland is deeply interested in Vitamin Therapy and is President of the British National Association for Health.

Bantam Book Catalog

Here's your up-to-the-minute listing of over 1,400 titles by your favorite authors.

This illustrated, large format catalog gives a description of each title. For your convenience it is divided into categories in fiction and non-fiction—gothics, science fiction, westerns, mysteries, cookbooks, mysticism and occult, biographies, history, family living, health, psychology, art.

So don't delay—take advantage of this special opportunity to increase your reading pleasure.

Just send us your name and address and 50¢ (to help defray postage and handling costs).